THEY SOLD ME

MACKENZIE HUON

CONTENTS

•BETRAYAL•

Cara's POV-

"Cut the shit Axel," I laugh as my little brother snatches the toast out of my hands.

It was nearing the end of my freshman year in the Lockwood Community College. I still lived with my family because we were poor.

I'll be able to change this. Don't worry papa, I'll do it for you, I thought.

My mother had died when I was born, so my papa was my only guardian. That was until my stepmother who is untrusting and her kind daughter were put into the family. However, even with the addition, papa was always there for me. He gave me so much love that inspires me even to this day to do well in school.

"Good morning Cara," a sappy voice rose up behind me.

I whirled around to see my older stepsister, Ana. She was extremely kind to me and helped me whenever I was in need. I hugged her, the warm scent of fresh strawberries embracing me. Her fiery red hair always contrasted with my dark brown hair.

My papa walked into the kitchen which was currently a mess because of Axel. He warmly smiled at me and quickly walked out the door looking clearly worried. I ran out to ask him what was wrong, but my stepmother gripped my shoulder.

"Child, eat your food. We don't want to waste it," she says snappish. "Right," I say a little distraught and I finish my toast.

I run upstairs and quickly jumble all my supplies and books into a bag. My dream one day was to become a doctor. Currently I was a second year med student with a bachelors in biology. I shove on a white tee and jeans while anxiously putting my hair up in a messy bun.

I run downstairs and kiss Ana and Axel on the cheek. I quickly wave to my stepmother who glared at me in return. I run out the door and walk to the bus stop. Yikes the old crow is never in a good mood. Then again, when is she ever, I think to myself as I sit on the unnaturally cold bench. I get on the bus that squeaked and shuddered when it arrived ready to start the new day.

During lunch, I meet up with a few of my friends, Dawna and Kevin. She was a cute little sweatshirt wearing girl, always having something to scowl about. Kevin was a tall basketball player with more love for food than his own girlfriend. We walk out to a nearby taco hut. Kevin voluntarily pays for my lunch in return that I tutor him for one of his upcoming tests.

"Girl how many days have you worn that shirt?" Dawna asks wrinkling her nose. I begin to protest, but the ringer on my flip phone cut me off. Kevin comes back, tacos in hand. I answer the call and I hear a happy voice on the other line, "Cara! Come shopping with me after school. I saved up so we both can get a dress," Ana almost shrieks. "Alright, see you then," I smile into the phone and end the call.

Dawna raises an eyebrow at me when I put the phone in my pocket. "Was that Ana? She gives me a weird vibe," she says uncertain. I dismiss her by shoving a taco in her mouth. Kevin begins laughing and we finish our lunches. I dread through my classes and finally slump out of my last period, happy that it is the weekend. Today I was extremely tired and I didn't know why.

All I'm looking forward to is sleeping and hanging out with Ana, I think happily. I decide to go to the bathroom before leaving and check out how bad I was looking today.

I push open the doors and stare into the mirror. All I saw was a tall brunette with hazel eyes. Her freckles were defined and splashed on her nose like a constellation. Her eyebrows clearly shaped and her jawline was rockin'. I feel kind of pretty today, I think to myself as I leave the college.

When I get home, I crash on the couch, my body immediately attaching to it like a bear on honey. "Silly get up, we have to look glam today," Ana says pouncing on me and cheek kissing me. "Can't we just sit here and eat food," I pout, hoping she would change her mind. She shook her head and dragged me to the family car. I spotted my stepmom in the drivers seat, clearly looking annoyed.

"Mom here is going to drive us to the mall," Ana says while staring at her. Why is Ana looking at her so intently? I shake the thought from my mind and sit in the car. We silently drive to the Lockwood Mall and get dropped off at the front. "Time to go in sis," Ana says while smiling. Her smile looked a little off though. Maybe it's just me. After what seemed like hours, our stepmom picked us up.

"Man I can't wait to sleep," I groan as I collapse into the car. When driving I notice that we missed an exit that would take us home. Ana seemed to notice and says hurriedly, "Don't worry silly, we are gonna try on our dresses." I nod, but when I glanced at her, I froze. She was smiling, but it wasn't her usually go happy one, it was almost creepy and devious. Never mind it. I'm probably just tired.

We eventually ended up at a mansion, beautiful and big. We park in front of it, with a fountain in the background. I stared in awe and gulp, "Why are we here? We can't afford this?" Ana smiles dimly and leads me out the door holding both of our dresses in one bag. Our stepmom hurriedly jumps out the door and tosses the key to a valet. She pushes me to the doors and we walk in. Wow. It's incredibly gorgeous. Look at all these paintings, the marble floor, and even the chandelier! Ana giggles and pokes me on the nose. A man in a suit approaches us.

"Hello madam, welcome to your stay. The guest will appear shortly. Please let me lead the way," his gruff voice echoes as he walks through one of the hallways. We follow him and he gestures toward a door. Inside, it is what seems to be a dressing room.

"Go on put on your dress. I'll put mine on too," Ana grins. I weakly smile, still confused by this sudden event. I pull out the white simple gown that seemed to cost much. I put it on and toss my hair into a bun. "Really now, you need to stop doing that," Ana says as she reaches for my hair. Is my hair weird in a bun? I've always had it up. She puts on a black dress fitted around her curves. "Wow-w you-u look stunning," I stutter.

She pushes me out of the doors and we again see the man in the suit. "This way ladies," he says with his voice lowered. He walks up the stairs into another dashing large room. "It's beautiful," I gasp, my eyes twinkling.

"Good evening ladies," a husky voice says behind us. I slowly turn around and I nearly fall. The man I see is so beautiful I'm at loss for words. His eyes are a deep grey, the color of cold silver. His hair was a peppery brown, longish as it is messily swept over. His jawline clearly defined and a stubble on his face. His body was... wow. His tight fitting dress shirt unbuttoned at the cuff, his muscles clearly shown through the shirt. His cigarette was dangling from his mouth and he looked at us coldly, but curiously.

He stares at me for a while, studying me and then finally speaks, "Claire, our deal is?"

She clears her throat and replies, "You may have this girl and in return we get money. It doesn't matter what you do with her." My blood ran cold. I swivel on her, "What the hell Claire? We never.. I would never.." Ana walks up to me and trails a finger under my chin. "Ana, please tell your mother she's crazy. Given that.. She's insane!"

She purred, "Oh Cara. If only you knew how much we hated you."
My heart shattered. What? How? I thought..I thought they loved
me? My own sister? She.. I was interrupted by a cutting edge voice.
"Claire, I agree to your offer. Men." The gorgeous man then flicks his
fingers toward us. The suited men surrounding him hands suitcase
to my stepmother.

She grabs it, her eyes showing greed and victory. Ana smugly laughs
and glares at me but sweetly. "Ana you bitch. How fucking dare you,"
I seethe in anger. She clicks her tongue, "No hard feelings. Pleasure
to make business with you Mr. Ethan Stone. Let me know if I can
do anything for you," she winks. "You are too crude for my taste. In
fact I find you uglier than most," the man I suppose is Ethan sharply
says. He motions for them to leave and they are escorted out. They
turn back one last time to see my reaction. I hold up my middle finger
toward them.

"My my? The rose has a thorn," Ethan whispers as he points my
chin up so I face him. I glare at him and I collapse, too overwhelmed
by these events. My vision getting hazier and then...blackness.

•A New Point Of View•

Ethan's POV-

"Shit," I grumble as I just barely catch the girl. I study her fair features and I move the hair in her face. I have no such need for her, but she could be useful. Even though she fainted, it didn't seem like she was scared. "Luis, grab Dr. Wilson. Mark, take the girl," I have business in New York. Luis falters and adds, "Agreed sir. Who do you want to watch her when she wakes?" I point at him in return and I walk out the doors, snatching my jacket off the hook.

Being the oldest son, the heir to my father's company, I must ensure that I get what I want to any extent. "Daniel, take me to the airport. I need to be there by four o'clock sharp." My driver nods and starts the engine. I stare out the window at the mansion where my mother used to live. I close my eyes, sleep embracing me.

"Sir, we are here. I shall take care of your belongings," Daniel says, abruptly waking me. We arrived at the air field where my private jets reside. The runway was wet, the sign that it had rained. "I'll see you soon. Say hello to your family," I say to him and toss him a roll of

100's. He bows and returns to taking out the suitcases. I quick walk toward the jet, my pulse humming in my ears.

As I walk into the jet, an arm slithers around my neck. Julia, the penthouse whore. "Mr. Stone, can I be of service to you," she purrs, pushing her cleavage together in her tight red dress. I scoff, "Really Julia, isn't enough that you slept with almost every man I know?" She breaths down my neck, looking at me with anticipation. "Get off," I growl as I shove her to the side. She opens her mouth to stay something, but I glare at her, clearly I'm not in the mood. I sit down and put in my earbuds, waiting for the plane to take off. I refuse to fuck a whore.

My mind then drifts off the girl. What was her name again? Cara? She was quite beautiful but lean and weak. She is not of my interest. I wonder if I should kill her or train her. I am lacking in assassins, but if the girl escapes, she could be a problem. She almost reminds me of someone. It's so painfully clear but foggy. Suddenly I feel a tap on my shoulder, Sir? A drink?" I grimly look at the wine bottle, too tired to talk. She notices and pours me a glass.

After I finished the wine, I fall asleep once more. This time it takes me back to a painful memory. I'm ten years old in the mansion my mom lived in. Outside the sun was shining and the harmonic sound of birds filled the air. "Ethan my child, come here," my mother whispers, her arms inviting. I smile and embrace her, I love her so much. She smelled of jasmine, her kind face and wispy hair was etched into my mind.

I frown, I suddenly felt hungry. "Mother, please make me your special cake," I laugh, throwing my arms around her. She smiles, "Of course my son. Don't eat too much. Your father will be home soon." I nod my head and follow her to the kitchen. Inside, the counters were made of marble, the cupboards etched with wooden hearts, the colors of white and a light pink so peaceful. She began to make her cake, a chocolate cake that she always made for me.

However her cakes took much time and before I knew it, it was dark. "I wonder why your father isn't back yet," she wonders out loud. Mother began to frost the cake, her eyes twinkling. She loved baking, especially for me. While she was busily humming to herself and almost finishing the cake, I stared outside the window in the kitchen.

The crescent moon was peering down on me, almost looking sad. The sounds of crickets filled the night, soothing me and my mind. Rustle. What is that? Maybe it's a dog. I dismiss the thought. Then again. Rustle. I frown and peer into the dark night, hoping to the find the source of the sound. Crash. I whip around, whispering, "Mother What is going on?" Her face looked drained and pale. She grabbed my arm and hauled me upstairs. As she dragged me, I look behind once more to see that the beautiful kitchen window I was looking through was now broken.

An arm protruded from it, my heart began to hammer. Ba-bump. "Get in here," she whispers, clearly scared. She locks the door behind us and she waits. "Go into the closet and hide behind this secret door. They must never find you," she says, a tear trailing down her cheek.

Ba-bump. She kisses me on the head and I am still dumbstruck. I am put into the little secret room and she shuts the door with a small smile. Ba-hump

I peer into the hole and I see my mother, who was arming herself with a knife, looking frightened and angry. The door is knocked down and I see three men enter the room. She advances and pounces toward them, her eyes a fury. Slashing the throat of one of them, she falls back. Again she parries and fights, but eventually she falls, a knife in her gut. "Search for the child," a low voice says. The sound of feet fade and the man who just spoke comes into view.

He kneels down and stares at my mother. "Hello Clarissa. You are quite the beauty like others said. Unfortunately your child will not be the successor. We will kill him. I'm sorry it had to end this way," the man sneers. I still cannot see his face. "You..will never find him Luka," she forces out, coughing out blood. Ba-bump. "Face it. It's over," the man sneers and looks directly at me.

I stumble backward and cover my mouth to keep myself from screaming. He walks over and throws open the closet door looking for the source of the sound. He searches around and I see his face. A long scar running down his right eye to his cheek. His long shaggy hair was messy and he was missing one finger. Frustrated that he couldn't find me, he turns toward my mother. She grimaced and glared at him. "The Aces want to give you their welcome," he whispers. Then he takes out of the holster, a gun. He takes off the safety and points it at her. She turns her head to make direct eye contact with me and gives me a small smile. Ba-bump

Then he pulls the trigger and I stifle my crying. I silently sat there as my mother's head softly went to the ground and gave one last breath before shuddering and was still. He walked out of the room and spoke as if he knew I was there, "Mark my words boy, I'll find you." I shudder awake. I stare at the New York scenery as it comes into view, my heart beating wildly. Ba-bump.

•CAPTIVE•

Cara's POV-

I wake in a soft mattress, my body feeling all the comfort there is. Last nights thoughts flooded into my brain and I sat up suddenly. I need to get out of here. I slide off the mattress but something in the window catches my eye. I walk to it, staring at the beachside that was extremely beautiful. Palm trees with a gorgeous green color, waves rolling lazily across the sand, and seagulls gliding above the waters. As expected of California, the scenery was all too perfect.

Wait a minute. This gives me an idea. Before I can move, I hear footsteps walking down what seemed to be a hallway outside my door. "Fuck," I mutter as I jump into bed, pretending to sleep. A low male voice curiously asks, "Sunshine you awake?" I squeeze my eyes shut and wait for the figure at the door to leave. "It's crazy Sam. The girl has been sleeping for 24 hours," he says flabbergasted. "Just let her sleep for one more hour then have Coletta wake her up," the voice I assumed was Sam says.

When they leave, I spring up from the mattress. I take in my surroundings: a desk with a chair, a bathroom, bed, window, and a closet with extra bedsheets. I grab the chair and nudge it under the door knob so it couldn't be opened from the outside. Damn I feel like I'm in a movie or a dream. I shake off my thoughts and start tearing my bedsheets in order to make a rope.

I checked the clock hanging on the wall. Good I've got 30 minutes. I rush to the bathroom and check each drawer. I see a pair of scissors, a small switchblade, a used toothbrush, and a sponge. I shove the switchblade in my pocket. I tie the rope end to the bed frame and I open the window carefully. How stupid. They left me in a room with a window that can open. After tying the rope, I toss the other end outside. I tug on it to make sure it could support my weight.

10 minutes left. Okay here goes nothing. I crawl out the window and inch down on the rope. The ground was all sand. I land heavily and I stare in awe of the palm trees that surrounded the mansion. I weave in an out of them, hoping not to be seen. Observing the beach, I notice several beach chairs and multicolored umbrellas. I look up at the window and I hear an audible, "Oh shit. Boss is going to kill us." A man peers out the window and I hide behind a big palm. "It looks like she's gone very far," Sam growls. Oh my God. I might die if I get caught..

Suddenly I spot some movement. There was someone sitting on one of the beach chairs. Judging by the wealth of this property, I assume this is a private area. I sprint toward the person, taking the switchblade out of my pocket. As I get closer, I realized the person was a man. He seemed a little familiar, but I wasn't going to take chances.

I flip the blade open and sneak towards him. I hold the blade against his neck tightly and growl, "Where is the exit of this property?" He tenses and after several moments, relaxes. "Why should I tell you," he asks with a curious tone. Because you might die if you don't.. "Look. I don't want to injure you, so please coopera-" The man grabs my weapon arm and yanks it away. He stands up and knocks me to the sand, his body on top of mine.

The blade fell out of my grasp and was several feet away from me. He holds both of my hands above my head and I realized this was the man previously...Ethan Stone. I struggle, but he's way too strong. His steel silver eyes look into mine and his face moves dangerously close.

He smells of cigarettes and vanilla, a comforting scent.. Get a grip Cara. The guy has you pinned. You could literally die right now and you're just drooling over him. "Sweetheart, I'm rather impressed," he smirks. I avert my gaze, "There's nothing I can do. Just let me go," I plead. He gets up, releasing me. Big mistake idiot. I run, at least I think I'm trying to but he gripped my wrist. Ethan sighs, "You really can't think I'm that daft." I notice his body then, his perfectly tanned muscles, the defined lines that couldn't compare to any of the marble sculptures in the museums. "Enjoying the view?" I snap out of the trance and I look away. He's still holding my wrist.

I begin to stutter, "I was just.. they.." He drags me back to the mansion. I helplessly follow him, protesting. "Sam, Kyle, you are both idiots," Ethan snaps as he walks through the doors. "I didn't think the girl was that smart," Sam says holding his arms up in defense. He was a redhead, freckles covering his whole face, but he was still handsome. He wore a jean jacket, a white tight tank top under it and beach shorts. Kyle slaps him on the head. He was a blonde blue eye typical heartthrob. "The girl is smart and pretty? A bonus," he grins.

"Guard duty tonight. Both of you jackasses," he sighs. Suddenly a beautiful girl wanders into the living room. She was auburn haired and had green eyes that shone like jade. "Coletta, keep an eye on her will you," Ethan says, rubbing his temples. "Sweetheart, if you escape one more time, you won't get an easy off. You are my property. Remember that," he coldly replies and struts off.

What the fuck. What an asshole. I roll my eyes, but I couldn't help feeling a bit frightened. "Girl come here. I need to fix you. But first, breakfast," the girl named Coletta says as she grabs my hand. We head towards the kitchen. Lovely.

•MAKEOVER•

Cara's POV-

••••Now on with the story••••

"So you tried to escape huh," Kyle says as I enter the kitchen. He leaned on the countertop, peering at me expectantly with his blue eyes. "Give the girl a break Ky. Her stepmom is practically a bitch and her sister is a snake. She's had a lot to go through," Sam says slapping the back of Kyle's head. Kyle nods in agreement and walks to pantry. "Sam, get the pancake mix. It should be on the drawer over... there," Coletta says pointing. "Kyle pokes his head out of the pantry, "Aw man. Coles can't we eat something else? At least ones made from scratch?"

Finally, I speak up curiously, "Wait you guys never had actual homemade pancakes?" Sam shook his head, "Sunshine, we are honestly the worst cooks in this house. Ethan sent the chefs away on a vacation and now we are left here to starve." I think for a moment and pipe up, "I can make them from scratch if you'd like," I offer, tossing the egg that someone had left on the table into the air.

Kyle runs up to me and hugs me, "Would you really?" I softly push him away and stutter, taken aback from the hug, "Y-yeah. I was the cook at my house.." my voice trails as I think of Papa and Axel. "Cheer up darling," Coletta says, "Besides, you have pancakes to make for 4 hungry children." "Don't label me as a child," a deep husky voice erupts from behind me.

I look behind me to see Ethan, who was wearing beach shorts and only a dress shirt...unbuttoned. Shit. I could get used to this view. His hair was messy, his muscles were defined, and he bore a large scowl on his face. Lighting up a cigarette, he noticed as I look away and he turns his attention to me. "Make the pancakes. I hate the mix right now," he says. "It wouldn't hurt to say please," I mutter, turning away. A hand grabs my arm and it's his. He forces me to look at him and he draws his face closer to mine. My heart begins to race. What the hell does he want. "Sweetheart, I don't say please," he says tilting his head a bit.

I panic and I push him off. "OkayfineIgotityessir," I yelp and I walk over to the pantry. When I look back at him, a bag of flour in my hands, he smirks at me and my heart does a somersault. "Eggs. I need eggs," I say, my face getting hot. "Ethan, you really fluster her," Kyle said amusedly. All of a sudden a wooden spoon hits him in the head. "Kyle, just shut up," Coletta says, retracting her arm.

I begin to make pancakes while Kyle proceeds to flirt with me and Ethan starts making omelettes for everyone. Once we set up the table, we eat. "Cara, what do you like?" Ethan asks. "Well.. I like art, baking, cooking, exercise, and boxing," I respond, shoving a bit of pancake in my mouth. "Boxing? How good are you at that?" Sam suddenly asks. "I developed extremely fast reflexes and I am able to defend myself, so I'm not sure." I suddenly see a sausage flying at me and I catch it, inches from my face. I'm confused. "What are you trying to do Ethan," Coletta asked, snorting and trying not to laugh.

Ethan ignores her and we continue eating. After we finish, she grabs at my arm and calls out, "Later, gonna dress her up a bit. Meet us at the pool in 30 minutes."

Coletta led me to a room filled with clothes I could only dream of. I gasp in awe. "Welcome to my place," she smiles obviously proud. Dresses from every color of the rainbow hung in color specified closets and mirrors, makeup, and chairs were lined up near the back of the room. "It's..beautiful," I stammer. These were clothes only I could dream of.

She grabs my hand and peers into my face. "Your eyebrows are in horrendous shape, your clothes are extremely unflattering, take off those silly glasses; haven't you heard of contacts? Also, you obviously have no experience with makeup and your haircut looks like it was done by your mother," she says. Uh what the fuck?

Before I could say anything, she places me on a stool and faces me toward her. "Listen darling, it won't hurt," Colette smiles apologetically as she holds up her tweezers. Wait a minute.. "HOLY SHIT,"

I shout as she begins to pluck every damn hair off my brow. "Yeah it hurts at first," she grins and continues. I proceed to cuss and shout for the next ten minutes. "What the hell did you do to my fucking face," I mutter angrily. I was not a happy camper.

"Now for makeup," Coletta said excitedly ignoring my remark. As she applied makeup, she murmured, "Darling I can't tell if you're stupid, brave or intelligent. Number one, trying to escape from a dangerous organization is definitely not what Einstein would've done. Number two, you certainly have guts to go against one of the most wanted men on this earth, and three, you obviously planned your escape well, at least until you met the boss." I glare at her, "What the hell was I supposed to do? If I'm trying to escape from the people that bought me, am I supposed to sit there and obey orders like a dog?"

She continues to apply more makeup and told me to shut up so she could put on some lip gloss. "If you think this is supposed to make me gorgeous, you are definitely blind," I mutter. "You have potential," she says studying me. "Look at yourself," she whispered and twirled me around. I dumbly looked into the mirror, "Who the fuck is this," I gasp in awe obviously knowing it was me. Why do I look decent? That's a first.

She walks away, leaving me to myself. Studying myself in the mirror, I also manage to continuously poke myself to see if I was dreaming. "Quit doing that. You look like an idiot," Coletta rolled her eyes as she tossed me a bag filled with clothes. "Go ahead, put them on," she smiles deviously. "Thank you," I quickly say and walk into a changing room.

Motherfucker. "Coletta, what the fuck is this," I call out. It's a damn bikini. "What you think it is darling," she sing-songs. It was black, like lingerie and it showed every curve I didn't know I had. I walked out clearly uncomfortable. "Wow darling, you look great," she says, her eyes lighting up. "I'm not going out like this," I snap. "Calm down tiger, I'm giving you this," she hands me a blanket. I raise my eyebrow at her and she begins to explain. "Look. Everyone knows you looked a little shabby. I invited everyone to the beach and then you can show them your makeover. Plus, don't worry about the makeup; it's waterproof," she says pushing me out the door.

I walk out, blanket completely covering me and the sun bathing me in light.

•INSANITY•

Author's note:Hi readers! I'm so sorry I wasn't able to update very fast:(I've got finals and stressful work going on..but I finishedwoohoo and I'm back:) love you all! Enjoy:)

- Ethan's POV -

I stand on the scorching ground, my feet buried in the sifted sand. I click my tongue in annoyance, I've been waiting for over twenty minutes. Where are those two. Sam was being buried in the sand repeatedly screaming while Kyle was tossing sand on him, giggling like a toddler. I touched my fingers to my temples. How the fuck can this organization survive? Hearing footsteps behind me, I swivel around, holding a cigarette in the corner of my mouth.

"You finally decided to join us Miss Cara?" She walks closer and I realize she's wrapped up in a blanket. I raise my eyebrows. What the fuck. It's like ninety degrees out. She nervously clutches it and walks slowly, taking no mind of the sand burning at her feet. I am going to get a kick out of this one. She stops in front of me and I glance at her face. Wait a minute.

Her face was like a new person. Her hair hung in wisps around her shoulders, her hazel eyes shone like topaz, her freckles splattered across her face like stars. She's beautiful....She's only a girl. Nothing worth your time. She's only a plaything. "You can stop staring now," a voice says dripping with sarcasm breaking out of my thoughts. I wrench her wrist up and bring her close to my face. "Not a chance. Just staring at how mediocre you are," I whisper in her ear, biting it.

Her face flushed, crimson meeting her olive tan skin. She shoves me off, clearly shaken and sand flies everywhere. I laugh deeply, "Now now..Is the kitten turning into a tiger?" She turns her head away, avoiding contact. Let's tease her a little more. I pull her body close to me, my hand at the small of her back. The only thing blocking it was the blanket. "God, it's a hundred degrees out. Get a grip," I grumble. She attempts to pull away from me, but she can't. She isn't strong enough. Feisty huh? I lift her chin and whisper, "What's under here?" Cara snaps in return, "Nothing. Let me go bitch." I see.

I release her as she fights back one more time and she flails into the sand. The sound of waves fills the air. The blanket had fallen around her and she was...stunning. Her perfect curves defined the black bikini. She sat there, her face red and she grabbed the blanket as if to cover herself. I step on it instinctively. What a sight. Before I could say anything, Colette jumps out of nowhere. "Quick to pounce?" I roll my eyes and walk toward the ocean.

Sam grins at me while holding Kyle in a headlock position. "You both are idiots," I smirk. Sam points to Kyle, who was protesting.

- Cara's POV -

How fucking outrageous this bastard is. He's fucking gorgeous and I can't do anything around him. I pick myself up and smile shakily at Colette, who happened to save me. "Sweetheart, you got seduced," she says smiling deviously. She runs to Sam, who was beating Kyle in wrestling. The last thing I heard within earshot was, "YOU IDIOT." I pat my face, my cheeks still red. I watch Ethan's perfectly toned back muscles swaying to the perfect rhythm of the waves. I gently touch my ear, feeling the reminisce of his bite. I stare at the ground, my heart hammering.

I brushed the sand off my thighs and elbows and walk towards them. "Oh shit," Sam said as he watched me walk towards them. Unfortunately for him, he had loosened his grip and Kyle wrangled free, immediately punching him in the nose. He groaned, "OH GOD. MY NOSE." Kyle laughed and walked toward me, his eyes sparkling. "Wow sweetheart you're a perfect ten," he murmurs. I blush, I never truly believed I was even close to beautiful.

We sat in a circle talking, lashing sand on each other and giggling like maniacs. Colette brought wine bottles and we started having a drinking competition. I could hold my alcohol really well. But, I went through many cups and in the end I became buzzed. The others passed out or were giggling randomly. I peered curiously behind me and saw Ethan sitting on the wet sand, the waves of water creeping towards him, but never succeeding. "I'll be back," I whisper drunkenly, Colette in response slumped forwards falling asleep.

- Ethan's POV -

"What brings you here, sweetheart?" My voice was deep, questioning, and sounding tired. "I.. just wanted to check up on you," Cara stammers, a drunken flush sitting on her face. She sits next to me, staring at the waves overlapping each other, a deep blue I thought was incomprehensible. I look over my shoulder and saw the boys drunkenly playing patty cake and Colette snoozing on Kyle's shoulders.

She speaks up, "I remember my mother. She was as beautiful as the ocean, calm and melancholy. I couldn't save her...when she had a heart attack. I held her hand as the police spoke to me, giving me directions. When I lost her, I felt like my world fell apart. I..We always went to the beach together. My footprints would intertwine with hers in the dampened sand," Cara say suddenly, tears slipping out of her eyes. "I'm sorry. I'm-" She never finished because I hugged her. Her pain was so evident in her words and she collapsed. Shit. Is she okay? Oh fuck.

I held her shoulders and a soft snore erupted from her. I snickered, she fell asleep. So pure. I let her lay her head on me and I stared at the ocean, thinking of my mother as well. Hours later, I carried Cara to her room and dragged the others home.

In the end, I couldn't stay away.

•ATTACK•

Cara's POV

"Aw fuck my head," I groaned getting out of bed. I wander to the kitchen where I see Ethan cooking breakfast. "You're up early." I wave at him dismissively, "I've got a fucking killer hangover," I groaned. He tosses a water bottle at me and I instinctively catch it, gulping in the contents. I pause and ask him, almost demanding, "How drunk were we?" He turns around and winks at me, "Enough for you to sob your life story." I sit at the table, head in hands. How humiliating.

Soon, Sam, Kyle, and Colette stumble into the kitchen, praising Ethan for his cooking skills. He knocks them on the head with his spatula and ordered them to sit. His wet messy hair was flung about his face, his eyes were piercing with silver, and his muscles bulged from his skin tight shirt, waiting to be released. For the first time, It almost felt like a family.

"Kitten eat your breakfast. We need to check our penthouse because of a recent attack. You stay here. I trust you enough because you obviously drunkenly sobbed your whole life story yesterday," he smirks, sending my heart beating into a frenzy. I glance at them, uneasy. "Don't worry, no one will hurt you," Colette smiles. "Besides we will only be gone for an hour." After the boys and Colette finished their omelettes, they rushed out of the doors.

I lock the metal door behind me and observe the house. It was a large home, filled with beautiful flowers. If I didn't see that it was a home, I would have thought it was a greenhouse. Plants loomed in every corner, luscious petals ripe with vibrant color, droplets of water dripping from the leaves, stems of healthy green. I glanced at picture frames. I saw Kyle and Sam as babies, both clutching each other in the photos. I spot Colette holding a What do I do now? Pose as she stands over dropped ice cream in another photo. I glance around the rooms, but I began to think of cookies. I'll bake some chocolate chip cookies. Remembering the list in my head, I start gathering ingredients.

Twenty minutes into the baking process, I hum to myself. I realized I was humming the tune, "You are my sunshine" and a tear slipped down my cheeks. My mother. She sang this to me...before the accident. I wipe my hand quickly over my cheek and shake the thoughts from my mind. After the cookies were out of the oven, I glanced at them, beautiful glazed chocolate chips melting in gooey dough.

The chocolate was oozing from...Crash. I whip my head around for the source of the noise. What the fuck was that? Are Sam and Kyle trying to joke with me? I hear a loud bang and unfamiliar voices. Before going downstairs, I caught a voice saying, "There's no one here I believe.." My heart begins to race and my mind thought back to when Colette said, "Don't worry. No one will hurt you." Bullshit. I have to hide. Now.

Worriedly, I grab a kitchen knife and head to my room, hiding. I wield it, my hands shaking nervously. Luckily there was a closet and I hid in it, my heart racing. Step. Step. Step. Pause. "Liam. You said there was no one in the house," a whining male voice said skeptically. I detected his voice in the kitchen. "Search the house," a low gruff voice commanded. Several other people rushed around the house, cautiously stepping into every room.

I calm myself down, forcing myself to breathe. Cara. They won't find you. You are going to be safe. I sat, waiting and footsteps weaved in and out throughout the house. Suddenly the door opened and I came face to face with a man. He was drop dead gorgeous. He had blonde dusty hair, a hard face, a scar running down from his right eye, and a tiger tattoo on his neck. He's beautiful. Shit. Cara you're so fucking stupid. He reached for me and I dodged, slithering behind him, holding the knife to his neck. His neck was warm, but his heartbeat was calm.

"So..This is Ethan's new whore," he says finally speaking. I reply sternly, "I am not a whore nor his woman. Leave this house and I won't hurt you." He touches the knife at his throat, "You are an interesting woman. Who are you?" I firmly hold the knife to his neck and his hands leave the knife, but still in the air. I say, my voice shaking, "That's none of your business. I said. Leave the house."

He suddenly wrenches my arm back and I drop the knife. Fuck. He turns toward me and I drop on the ground, grabbing for the weapon.

He steps on it. He begins to laugh, "I am Liam, Ethan's rival. Should I take his woman or kill her myself?" I tremble, moving back on the wall. "Don't touch me," I plead. He smirks and inches closer to me and I move back with his every step. He hums rhythmically, "You are interesting. I wonder. How good are you in bed?" Outraged by this comment, I backhand slap him. Oh shit. I'm probably going to die now. Instead, Liam smiles, danger reflecting in his eyes. "You have more than what meets the eye." He grabs my face and yanks it up to look at him. He slowly goes in...for a kiss. I shut my eyes, waiting for it to be over.

"You bastard," a voice growls behind him. Liam moves with me to the side as a bullet hits the wall to where he was. I look behind me. Ethan. Thank God. Ethan stands there, covered in blood. His eyes seething with hatred, a gun in his hand. Liam clucks disapprovingly, "Ethan, I met her. She's quite beautiful and feisty. Don't you think a man like me should have a woman like this?" Ethan growls, his handsome face twisted in such anger. I've never seen him so upset. "Don't touch Cara." Liam smiles, "I suggest you put the gun down."

It only riled up Ethan, but guns click, the safety off. He is surrounded, Colette stood behind him, bloodied and out of breath. Guns were directed at her. Sam and Kyle were passed out, clearly beaten up. Tears welled in my eyes. Liam glances at my face, "You cry? Perhaps I will..give them mercy. However, they killed most of my men. That needs consequences." I face him, "Please. Don't hurt them," I beg. Tears are falling. How humiliating. "Release them. We can kill them another time. I admire their capability to kill. I'll be back for you love." He kisses my hand gently and walks out past Ethan.

They soon leave, the door closing with a faint click. I rush to Ethan falling into his arms. "Don't let them. Please." He holds me back, whispering, "I promise."

·Soft·

A uthor's note: Hey lovesI put in different male pictures just to give you an idea what the character looks like:) of course you can just leave it to your imagination enjoy loves

Ethan's POV

I held her. I don't know why. Cara looks up at me, her hazel eyes wide with fear. Did that bastard.. "Did he hurt you?" She shakes her head, her wispy hair in a halo and separates from me. I turn to follow her as she hurriedly makes her way towards Sam, Kyle and Coletta. I kneel down, holding Coletta. Her beautiful face was badly bruised, bones obviously broken and her arm bent at an unnatural angle. How could this happen? Utmost..Why didn't he kill them? I picked her up and walked to her room. She was out cold.

When I came back after tucking Coletta in her bed, Cara was sitting the boys upright and they were groaning with weak smiles. Sam's right eye was shut, his chest bleeding and his legs had gashes in them. Kyle leaned on Cara's shoulder and he suffered the most out of all of us. "Cara, the med kit is downstairs. On the top shelf," I say curtly.

She nods and runs downstairs, footsteps pounding the floors. Sam hoarsely whispers, "Before you say anything Ethan, I know why he kept us alive. Before you came into the house, we saw Liam and his men breaking into the house. We immediately attacked but his men returned our advances. Because we attacked them, they gave us a beating, but explained why they came. Ace has returned." Ace. Ace Conan.

"I will fucking rip his face to shreds. I will do anything to kill him," I growl, my teeth clenched. Mother I will avenge you. Your life will not have been wasted. "We need to form an alliance with Liam," Kyle murmured, his arm shaking to support his weight. He peers at me with his swollen and battered face. "No way in hell. No fucking way. I will not ally with him," I say coldly. "What can you do? Ace has too many reinforcements around the globe. Plus, he's still hunting you. Your reinforcements are all the way in New York," Sam says coughing blood into his sleeve.

Cara returns, holding a bag. "I'm back. I organized the supplies," she says breathlessly. "No need, I will call a doctor," I say, eyebrows raised. "I'm mostly a doctor. If you call one, it'll only bring attention to this event," she says determined. "Show me what you can do," I challenge. While she whips out bandages, gauze, ointment, rubbing alcohol and needles, I watch her curiously. She has heart, but she's worthless. Defenseless. What can I do with her? "Ethan. Teach me to fight and use weapons," a small voice said interrupting my thoughts. Sam and Kyle passed out, exhausted from the fighting and their injuries.

"Can you handle killing a person," I ask, ready for her to say she couldn't. "I can. I've been training to be a doctor my whole life. I can give life, but I can take it too." She stands up, her clothes covered in blood. Her eyes, colorful and determined. She's fucking gorgeous.

- Cara's POV -

He stood there, studying me; my gestures, my features, my mind. Ethan was wearing grey joggers, but they were hanging low that I could see the etched lines of his muscles defining his v-line. He wore a tight sweatshirt. Again. Why are his muscles so captivating. He cocked his head, thinking of how to answer my request of fighting. His beautiful face carved out in a worried manner, his face etched with curiosity. Oh fuck. He's irresistible. His body...His face..His murderous tendency.

Breaking through my clouded thoughts, I realized Ethan was in front of me. I looked up at him, blinking in confusion. His expression was...soft. Ethan grabbed my hand and led me to the other side of the house. He tossed me into this room. His...office? "You are so fucking beautiful Cara." He says holding his head to mine. I breathlessly stare at his lips, my heartbeat racing.

"May I?" He asks in a low seductive voice. It makes me shiver and I press my lips to his, as an answer. His kiss was aggressive, but gentle. His lips pressed on mine and he began to hold me closer, his hand on my waist. "You smell good," Ethan whispers hoarsely as his fingers crawl up my chest. His hands moving under the fabric that covered it. I in return did the same, feeling his every sculptured line. He kisses my neck and I whimper a small moan. I clamp my hand over my mouth. Shit.

He smiles deviously, "Music to my ears." I flush red, taking off his sweatshirt revealing his large chest. He unbuttons my shirt, his face still buried in my neck. After it's off, he grabs my ass, biting my ear and making me go...crazy. He slams me to the wall, his kisses going lower and lower. I try to push him away, but he grabs my hands and holds them over my head.

Oh my God. He's so good. I can't.. I can't stop. Ethan unclips my bra with one hand. How many times has he done this? He starts kissing lower and lower, my chest spotting with hickeys. Holy shit.

·Toy·

Author's note: Hey guys! I'm back:) I can't believe I have so much support from y'all :) thank you so much!

-Ethan's POV-My fingers traced along the small of her back. So damn soft. She shivers slightly and I pull her even closely towards me. The way her face looked. Made me want to devour her. Such a desire she is. Her face is flushed red, her eyes sparkling and ..daring. Get ahold of yourself Ethan. A woman? She surely is mediocre compared to others... "Ethan, don't stop," she breathes in my ear. Any doubts were cleared from my mind and I continued, the night becoming more refreshing the lower my hand creeped down her body.

Before I knew it, it was morning. Fuck what time is it? What about the others? I attempt to move but I feel this weight on me. I glance down. Ah...There she is. An angel.. Her face was buried in my arms. I brushed the tufts of hair from her golden face. The one who saved me.

-Cara's POV-I woke up with a start. Woah. This isn't my bed... Memories from last night flooded my head. I cover my face with the satin red sheets that covered Ethan's bed. It smells just like him.. A smoky scent. My face was red with embarrassment. But.. I don't regret it. That's the weird part. "That didn't just happen," I murmur into the sheets. I slide off the bed, the sheets covering my erm.. unclothed front side.

I attempt to sneak out, my arm brushing the side of the walls for support. I don't look back and I grab the red silk robe that hung on the peg of the bed. I slide in on, glancing at Ethan's sleeping face. So gorgeous.. beautiful but dangerous... I tiptoe to the door. I sigh with relief as I reach the door, a white painted wood with a picture frame. A picture of a beautiful tall woman with brown hair clutching a young child. Is that...Ethan? I shake my head and put my hand on the doorknob.

The door opens silently and my face lights up. All of a sudden... a hand slams the door shut. Ethan stands behind me, his other arm beside me. I turn around abruptly. "Where you going? I didn't say you were done," he smirks. His grey eyes stared right into mine. He glanced down at me. I was disheveled; my hair with it's messy curls and the bathrobe falling off my shoulder. He stares at my bare shoulder.

I bite my lip and look away. I'm so nervous. "Don't do that you little seductress," he murmurs. He tilts my face toward him and he heads straight for my bare skin. He sucks my neck and the feeling of ecstasy shoots through me. I moan a little, making him suck even more. His arms hold my body and he bites me. I moan even more and I feel him with my hand. He's so big right now. I undo his belt and slide down his pants.

He pauses and his eyes glint at me just as a predator would do with his prey. I gulp and he slams me into the wall. He kisses me furiously and I kiss him back. His lips caressed mine and I bit it. So good.. I can't stop. He stops and moves his head down to my breast.

As I wrap my legs around him, he smiles into my skin. I want him. I-need him... He slides it in and I moan into his ear. "God if I had known about you earlier...You would have been mine from the start," he musters out. I couldn't talk. My head was filled with lust.

-Ethan's POV-

Shit. How could this woman of mediocrity make me fall in such a state. There's something about her. It makes me go wild. Every damn moan and every damn move she makes just makes me want to hold her. I see her face, obviously enjoying every moment. I loved it.

I gave her everything I could. I laid her on the bed, slowly fingering her delicate body. She was perfect. When she finished, she shivered and moaned with such a voice. God it was amazing. Cara. You are mine.

ENCOUNTERS

Author's Note: Hey guys! I was planning on leaving the story here. After all, these are just my 1AM shenanigans. However, I have been receiving many messages about resuming the story:) Since we are all quarantined, I will be more active. To those who are suffering losses to this virus or are scared. We are all in this together. We will overcome this:) (P.S. the guy above is Sam) (P.P.S. I made this an extra-long chapter :))

-Cara's POV-

I know I know..I'm wearing a skimpy shirt and I smell of sex. I totally forgot about Sam, Coletta, and Kyle. I've been so selfish. Just thinking about my desires... I race out of Ethan's bedroom. I fee; his piercing grey eyes stare me down as he leaned against the doorway. I shove open the door leading to Sam and Kyle's room. I breathed a sigh of relief. They're still sleeping. I gaze at the pale white walls encircling the boys. What filled the walls were posters of football players and....half-naked girls. I roll my eyes. Childish. I stare at the clay bowl sitting on their nightstand. It was filled with water with a twinge of red. Blood. I shake my head of the thoughts. I take the dishcloth on Kyle's forehead and dip it into the shockingly cold water. "Cara?"

I whipped my head around and saw Kyle groggily shake this head. I turned my head towards Sam. He was out cold. I smile, "Hey Kyle. How are you feeling?" He weakly returns the smile and whispers, "I'm better than I thought. Treat Sam first. His injuries are worse than mine. I'm going to go get some cereal and check up on Coletta." I nod and get on the bed. Sam was soundly sleeping his red hair fallen over his eyes. I held his face and tilted it, pressing the cool washcloth on the deep cut. I never noticed how his freckles were like a constellation on his face. All of a sudden Sam's eyes open abruptly.

"Sa-" I started to say, but his fierce glaze didn't recognize me. He flips me over on the bed and his arm hold my arms above my head. His body was inches away from mine. His leg between mine. I turn red, embarrassed, "Sam it's me. Cara." He wipes his eyes with his free hand. "Shit sorry. I've been having nightmares about the incident," he admits. Sweat beads his head. I lay there, my eyes betraying me.

"Damn, Cara. You look kinda cute like that," Sam says interrupting my thoughts. I realized my face was burning and he was 1 inch away from my face. Obviously he was enjoying this close encounter. "Alright Sam. Stop using your injuries as an excuse to be horny," Kyle says walking into the room. I struggle to leave Sam's grasp. He loosens his grip and I jump out of it. Oh my God.

"Y-you guys seem fine," I stammer shakily and jumping off the bed, "I'm going to go check up on Coletta. Oh and Sam?" He looks over at me curiously like a puppy. I throw the dishcloth at his face. It made a satisfying slap. I sniff and walk out the door. I could hear the roaring of laughter echoing the hallways.

I feel a hug behind me. "Coletta," I smile. She grins, a bandage wrapped around her eye, "Of course. Your one and only. How are the boys?" I roll my eyes, "Please. They're so annoying like always. They seem fine though," I say walking towards the kitchen. Dear Jesus

Ethan is here, making an omelet. I watch him carefully cut tomatoes, his hands softly grasping the knife. His back muscles move as he reaches on the shelf for salt. Coletta follows my eyes. She nudges me. "You got terrible taste," she murmurs playfully. I pretend to not hear. Ethan's scooped the vegetables into the pan. Carefully, he slides the omelet onto the dish. Whatever. Cara, he's just a pretty boy. Nothing special. Coletta whistles, "Ethan." Before he could turn, I panic and turn away. She smirks, shoving me onto him and immediately leaves the room. I crash onto his muscular back. Slowly he turns and looks down at me. Fuck fuck fuck fuck

"Cara," he says in a seductive voice. My heart races and I take small steps backward. "You smell nice," Ethan says wrapping his arms around my waist. My thoughts race. His face buries into my neck. "I-I have to go um...check up on Sam and Kyle," I stammer. He whispers in my ear, "No. I'm not finished with you yet," and his fingers slide up under the shirt. His hair smells of faint smoke and vanilla. I push him off and swallow nervously. I run away and shut the door behind me. I face the door, my eyes closed and my head hitting the door repeatedly.

"What's wrong with me," I murmur. "Do you typically do this all the time?"

I swivel towards the voice. It's him. The man with the tattoo. Liam. He stood there, smoking a cigarette. His sharp eyes gazed over me in annoyance. I hit the door with my back in surprise. Quickly, I turn around trying to open the doorknob. Ethan! "Now don't do that," he says, his hand slamming the door in front of me. I face him and I open my mouth to scream. He growls and slaps his hand over my mouth. "Look gorgeous. I don't have time for this. You're coming with me. If you scream I will slit your throat," Liam says, his hand dropping from my mouth. A knife emerges from his pocket and it flicks open. "I won't yell. But I won't come with you," I say scornfully. He smirks at me, his face getting dangerously close. "I never asked you. I said you're coming with me."

"Cara. Are you in your room?" A deep voice asks outside my door. Ethan. "Ethan here. Please hurry!" I burst out. Liam strikes my face and I fall, dizzy with pain. Ethan slams the door open and his eyes seethe with anger. "Did you fucking touch her?" Liam laughs and bends to hold my head, his knife held against my throat. "I said. She's coming with me." Ethan growls deeply, "She's mine. Understand that, fucker?" Liam holds the knife closer to my neck. "You know. She's quite pretty..and smart. I did my research. Cara Liss Evangeline. Daughter of Christopher Robin and current med student. Step-mother and sister are hateful towards her. Her father is falsely told that Cara died in a car accident. However, Miss Evangeline here may not even be related to Christopher at all.." I turn slightly, wide-eyed.

"What do you mean?" Liam turns towards me, amusement in his eyes. "Evangeline, you may be the possible daughter of the man Ethan is trying to kill." "Enough. You will let her go now. I own her," Ethan says, his eyes narrowed and his hands trembling with anger.

Liam loosens his grip and smirks at Ethan. "Really now. Did you fall in love with this girl already? Weren't those penthouse whores not enough for you?" I take this chance and bite his hand and he grunts in pain. I fall out of his grasp and his arm heads towards me. Ethan rushes forward and pulls me in, his knife pointed at Liam. "No worries. I'll take her next time." He stands up and jumps out the window. I rush to the ledge, but he was gone.

BURST

Author's note: Enjoy this picture of Coletta:)

-Ethan's POV-

Goddamn it. I need to stop being so damn soft. I stare at Cara. Her baby blue shirt slowly ruffles against the soft wind. Wisps of brown hair fly around her head like a crown. She looks over at me, slowly turning around. She gives me that smile, her head tilted. Her hands are trembling. I walk towards her not knowing what I'm about to do. She moves back slowly, her eyes trained on me until her waist hits the window ledge. She starts tipping over. What the hell is she doing? Wait. Shit shit. I see her arms flailing wildly as she tips out the window. I run forward her arm poised towards me. Almost there... got it. She's halfway across the window, my arm holding hers.

She gasps faintly and I realized that our waists were touching. Half her body outside the window, dangerous to the fall. Her luminescent eyes stared at me curiously and nervously. I held her arm and kissed it. I peer closely at her and breathe, "You can't escape me that easily."

-Cara's POV-

Such a gorgeous face. It was like being in slow motion. I almost fell... His arm grabs mine and he stares at me. No..my lips? Why does he do this? I-I can't thin-. He stopped my thoughts with a kiss. Desire shoots up through me and I furiously kiss him back. He's warm. It's nice.. It's been a while since I've been hugged like this. It almost.. reminds me of mom...He holds me, his arms wrapping around my body. Oh god. Why am I crying? I turn away in shame. In the last three years, I had never cried. So why now? Suddenly, a gentle hand turns my chin up. Ethan. His gaze was soft, his eyes-instead of dark thunderstorms were soft and puffy grey clouds. He murmurs, "What's wrong Kitten?" He wipes the tears from my face.

"Ethannn. Why is there only one omelet?" A playful voice says outside of the door. It's Sam. I can't let them see me like this. It's so humiliating. Ethan moves towards the doorknob. I instinctively grab his shirt, "Ethan." He peers at me and nods with understanding. Gently, he pushes me behind the door. "What do you want?" Ethan gruffly says. "Aw don't be like that Tan Tan. We need our expert chef back in the kitchen," Sam laughs. "Sure sure. I'll be there," Ethan says clearly annoyed. After Sam left, Ethan closes the door and hugs me. Then he left too. What am I going to do with these feelings?

I walk to the kitchen, playing with the lone string on the broken seam of my shirt. "Here's our little sexy vixen. Come eat," Coletta says winking at me, her mouth full of omelet. Her auburn hair was in a tight ponytail and she was wearing red plaid PJs. Her eyes were glimmering from the ecstasy of the food. I smile as if my crying fiasco never occurred, "Good morning. Are you all well?" Kyle knocks me on the head and hands me the plate. "Here's for your hard work." I hug him and turn around to see Ethan..glaring at me. What the fuck did I do?

I sit down at the creaking oak table. Ethan finally sits down, poised and ready to attack his egg. Before his fork touches the egg he looks up. "Listen. Today (Friday) I am going to meet with an old friend. Sam and Kyle, I need you to teach Cara the basics of weaponry. I have to make several..deals on Sunday. So, I need everyone to be prepared and well dressed. I won't be back for several days."He takes his plate with him and walks out of the front door. I stand up suddenly,

"Wait, Ethan. Where are you going?" He stares at me coldly, "Like I said. I'm going out for several days." What the hell is this attitude? I angrily yell, "Ethan you can't just leave! What about Coletta, Sam, and Kyle? They're still injured!" He walks up to me and whispers harshly, "This doesn't concern you. You're just a mediocre girl who wants attention all to herself. Get off my ass." Damn. I could feel myself deflating.

He walked out the door. Everything was quiet. "Cara. Don't mind him. He's just moody," Sam says grimly. "Sure. Don't worry about him. We will teach you assassination," Kyle says grinning evilly. I weakly smile and stay quiet. He's never snapped like that before. After breakfast, I followed Coletta to a shabby grey door behind the stairs. Coletta lights up a cigarette before digging into her shirt to find a necklace with a key. She took it and unlocked the door. It opened with a creak. Kyle and Sam went below and we all ended up in a dark room. Coletta's cigarette lit up her face and she sighed, "Ugh, where's the light? Sam make yourself useful and find one will you?" "Dammit, I'm trying nerd," Sam mutters under his breath.

All of a sudden the room lights up. The walls were covered with dark sheets of metal. Dummies with targets on their heads were filled everywhere and a wall of weapons hung on the other end of the room. "Welcome to the training room." I gaze at the weapons.

I walk to the wall and stare at them. Assortments of guns, knives. Coletta comes up next to me and leans her arm on me. She asks curiously, "What do you prefer to use?" I look at the knives, my heart beating wildly. My hand runs over them, feeling the hilts and the knife surface. Coletta smiles, "Ah. So you like silent killers. I agree. Do you know what you want?" I tilt my head towards her, "No. I'm not exactly the most decisive person." Coletta touches several of the knives. Some were crested with jewels, some were just normal with wooden hilts.

"You don't strike me as the super fancy type," Coletta says while humming and stares at them. I pick up a knife with a jade hilt. The blade was a dark metal and it was so sharp that when I touched it to my skin, a crimson drop of blood appeared. "I like this one," I murmur while staring at it.

Coletta taught me the history and the materials of the knife. Kyle taught me how to gut an opponent within close range and Sam taught me to throw the knife from a long-range. This occurred several times a day for the next few days. I wonder what Ethan is doing... Before I knew it, Sunday came around and Coletta had woken me up early. She was more serious than she had ever been. Something is coming.

PREPARATION

A uthor's note: Here's a sample picture of Ethan;)
-Ethan's POV-

"Ethan. Do you have the cash?" My thoughts snapped back to reality. "Old man you're too greedy. Patience," I growl a cigarette in the corner of my mouth. I snap my fingers. Two of my men dressed in suits immediately surged forward. Each holding a briefcase full of cash. Being in this dusty warehouse was suffocating. I miss her. Even I can't stay away. I do regret saying such harsh things. I'll get to see her tonight though.

I sigh and stand up from the creaking chair, "So where are the men you offered me, old man? I trust that you properly trained them?" The old man, Mr. Shishunaga, was an old Indian man. He is superb at his assassination skills and his teaching of them too. Every month, I lose a few men, so I must buy some from this man. We are good allies and we provide each other with what we need. "Of course, brat. What do you take me for?" He clucks disapprovingly. However, a few of his students are always from rival gangs and try to kill me at every moment. What a damned pain. It'll happen soon too. "Davud, lead these men back to the base," I say while checking the time. 12pm. The party starts at 8pm. "Yes sir," Davud says and hands plane tickets to the newbies. They are being stationed in Ohio. Where recent attacks of...Ace. Forget it now. Fuck that bastard.

"Excuse me sir, but we need to talk to you privately," a young man with frizzy blonde hair said. He was with two other plain looking men. Oh? These must be the ones I expected. Davud told me earlier that three men were waiting to kill me from the Slithertooth gang. A pathetic excuse for one. They kill numerous women and children for their satisfactory gain. Anyone weak who opposes them dies. "Very well. You have ten minutes. Speak," I say amusedly. I lead them to the hallway behind the cargo.

Instantly, they pull out their knives. "Mr. Hiro said you were tough. You just look like a pretty boy to me," the blonde one sneers, taking a knife from his pocket. It had a crimson hilt and a ruby in the middle of it. The metal was sterling silver. "That's a nice knife. Maybe I should take it home to Cara," I say amusedly. "Who the fuck is Cara? Whatever it doesn't matter. Prepare to die," the other man says. A scar runs down his face to the nape of his neck. They all take knives from their pockets. "Pathetic. Go ahead. Try me," I laugh.

The blonde one charges me while the other throws his knife at me. Interesting. I dodge the knife and leap to the right. He follows my movement and launches himself at me. Fool. I duck down and grab his waist. Given that, I slam him on his back. He erupts in coughs. There's no cheating or rules when you are fighting for your life. At this point, it is survival and sense. The other puts up his fists. Street fighting style. Hold on. Where's the other one? I swear there were three of them. I glance behind me to see a knife heading for my throat. Fuck. My guard is off. I drop to the ground and use my feet to knock the surprised bitch to the ground. He struggles to get up, but I immediately slit his throat. I lash out harshly, "Boring. You are truly a Slithertooth-predictable and slow."

"Shut up bastard!" the blonde yells, getting up. The other two men stand together ready to rush me. I check my watch. Damn. 6:00pm. I'm late. I take out the gun in my suit and shoot at the one with the scar. He falls instantly as a bullet hole forms in his head. I throw my gun at the blonde one. He winces and I take this opportunity to punch his gut. He groans, "We will defea-", "You are all pain in the asses," I interrupt and shoot him in the head. The scarlet red puddle flows towards my shoes. The bitter and arid aroma of blood rising in the air. "I'll take your knife though. I am quite fond of it." I pick up the fallen crimson knife and wipe the blood on my pants. I place it in my pocket, thinking of her. Damn my suit is a mess. "Davud. Take care of this mess and call the hotel. Tell them I'll be arriving soon," I mutter. "Yes sir."

-Cara's POV-

"What's wrong Coletta?" I ask as I notice her furrowed brow. I was groggy as I was just waking up in the morning. "We have a busy day ahead of us. Ethan didn't notify us until earlier this morning. He is planning to assassinate someone at the gala. We all have roles; even you darling," she says with a delighted tone. I could sense her desire of bloodthirst. "What is my role?" I say sitting up immediately in bed. She didn't say anything and took me by the hand. We went to the kitchen to have breakfast. I rubbed my eyes. Ugh, I really do feel dead. Especially after all that training. I doubt I'll be given an actual good role. Sam and Kyle were there already ravaging the fridge for food. Coletta smacks them both, "Oh God, what are you guys doing?" Sam looks at her teary-eyed, "Coco, there's no food!" I laugh and start taking supplies out of the fridge.

"Don't worry boys, I'll make crepes and cut some fruits," I smile. They cheered and sat at the tables like little puppies. While pouring batter into the pan, I thought of Ethan. I felt a pang of guilt and anger. Who is he to tell me off like that? Mediocre? I'll tell him! "Cara". I don't want to see him ever again. He's a fucking pain in the ass. "Cara!" I shake out of my thoughts. "Coletta?" I ask. "You're stirring the batter too much," she says poking me on the nose. She's right. The batter has gone everywhere.. "Anyways. Cara. You have a big role tonight. You are going to be known as the "Scarlet Fang". This is a cover to hide your true identity. Your goal is to pretend to be Ethan's wife and-" I hold my hand to pause her. "I'm sorry. Did you say wife?"

She smirks at me, "Yes. Technically it is true, but you both are too "scared" to share your actual feelings. Anyways. Kyle and Sam are going to pretend to be your bodyguards. This gala is extremely important to Ethan. There are five targets we must get rid of. One: Mr. Smith, a leader of a drug organization that assisted the Aces in murdering Ethan's mother. Two: Ms. Alisha, his wife who planned

out the attack on Ethan's mother. Three: Mr. Kim, the grandson
of the leader of Slithroats, a dangerous organization who kills major
political figures. He overthrew his grandfather and father and killed
them with his bare hands. Four: Mr. Tokishino, an assassin who
has direct links with the Aces. Five: Mr. Taki, a fashion model who
seems to be a threat to our organization. He is unpredictable and
shows signs of being an ally or not. If he cannot be our ally he is too
dangerous to leave alone. So far, I will take care of Ms. Alisha. Sam
and Kyle with Mr. Kim and Mr. Tokishino. You will meet with Mr.
Taki while Ethan deals with Mr. Smith."

"I see. I'm not sure if I'm prepared for all that," I admit. "I don't
think I could even be convincing at all." Coletta smiles, "Don't worry.
We will review the plan over and over." I head back to my room and
sit on my bed. Tonight is going to be awful. I might die. What am I
saying? I fall into a deep sleep, my worries slowly filling my head.

"Cara. It's time," a soft voice says. I nod myself awake and pull
myself from the bed. "Come with me," Coletta says as she leads me to
her room. I forgot she was a master of disguise. I spot Kyle and Sam
fixing themselves up in the mirror. They were wearing white suits
with black bowties. Their hair was slicked back and their faces grim
and serious. They were silent. I enter the room, remembering the last
time I was there. Somehow Coletta knows how to make me pretty.
It's amazing. "Alright, Scarlet Fang. Let's make you look the part," she
smiles. I sit on her bed, waiting. She comes out with a crimson gown
and a small belt. "Put these on. The belt is for your knife." I put on
the tight-fitting dress and I felt like Jessica Rabbit, but the top was

long-sleeved and it revealed a large cut of my back. Coletta then did
my makeup and put in my earrings. However, these earrings were not
just normal ones, but inside had little pellets of poison that dissolve
in any liquid. It has no taste nor smell. I looked in the mirror. Wow.
Is that really me? "Stop being so narcissistic," Coletta teased as she
slid up her black dress to put a holster for her gun. We met the boys
in the living room. The tension was in the air.

"You look great Cara," Sam says wide-mouthed. I smile in return
and we go out the door. I haven't been out in ages...The sun is going
down. The mood is silent and dangerous. We ride separately. I ride
with Sam and Coletta and Kyle ride together. We take two cars. One,
a sparkling white Bentley and two, a white Ferrari. Sitting in the
car, Sam explains the plan to me in great detail. We arrive at a lush
clubhouse that is larger than a mansion. People in gowns and glory
spill out from the building. Cars of high-status get out in front of the
building. Classical music echoes in the air. Valet parking boys take
our keys and we step onto enemy territory. Heels or dress shoes. We
have a long night ahead of us. I'm sure Ethan has arrived as well..

 - Ethan and Cara's POV-

 I'm ready

PARABELLUM

Author's note: Here are the targets and assassins matched:) Just so you don't have to go back to the next chapter (Oh here's Cara in her dress:)

Ethan: Mr. Smith, a leader of a drug organization that assisted the Aces in murdering Ethan's mother.

Coletta: Miss Alisha, the wife of Mr. Smith and the planner of the attack on Ethan's mother. Coletta has been ordered to give her the most painful death ever.

Sam: Mr. Tokishino, an assassin who has direct links with the Aces. He is always surrounded with armed men and can only be accessed by VIP.

Kyle: Mr. Kim, the grandson of the leader of Slithroats , a dangerous organization who kills stable and major political figures. Kyle is pretending to be his ally.

Lastly, Cara: Mr. Taki, a fashion model who is an unknown threat. No one knows if he is an ally or an enemy. He is too dangerous to leave alone.

- Ethan's POV-

I stepped onto the fresh grass. Damn. Smells like murder. I smile and weave my way into the clubhouse. I toss the keys to the valet boy. He catches it instinctively, the little red cap on his head catching the wind. I feel for the weapons in my coat. Good. Tonight will be tough. I stand at the door. I feel it over with my fingertips. Every crevice, carved line, and encrusted gold was right there. I push the door open, anticipated for the night.

-Cara's POV-

I walked through the doors, my arm looped with Sam's. Coletta's with Kyle's. We are silent, ready for the mission. As soon as we enter the doors and closer to the sound of violins, we disperse. Coletta gets a slight glint in her eyes and she drops Kyle's arm. She heads for the white marble stairs, her eyes focused on a woman wearing a golden gown. That must be.. Miss Alisha. Kyle heads off in the opposite direction, nodding towards us. He heads towards the pool tables-billiards. He's tense. I can tell by his hands in his pockets. Paranoia. I had stopped moving. "Sam?" Sam stares at me and whispers, "I have to go now. You know what to do." He drops my arm and heads off. I look around. What a lavish and beautiful place. Honestly.. my mind and my wallet are crying. I follow the music and enter a beautiful room with a bar and several candlelit tables. Such high status. So many people...

I walk in the bathroom. It was insane how pretty it was. Even the fucking soap dispenser is made of gold. Don't get distracted dumbass. I open my wallet and take out the small photo of Mr. Taki. God.

What a beautiful man. His jawline was sharp, his curly black hair swept to the side. His eyes were..green. Like my jade knife... "I never imagined that I would have a fan who follows me to the bathroom," a voice says over my shoulder. I freeze up and turn towards the voice. It's him! The man in the picture. I stare at the photo and then back at him. "S-sir. This is the women's bathroom," I stammer. Well, I just fucked this whole mission up. His face gets closer to mine and his hands land on the sink on each side of me. "Princess. This is the men's room," he says daringly. What? I look around and I see a sad little urinal sit in the corner. Ohmygodohmygodohmygod. He teases the toothpick that sits on the side of his mouth and opens his mouth to speak. I shove him to the side and shriek, "Sorry!" I run out the door, going into the correct bathroom this time.

I stand in the stall, observing the picture and touching the knife through the dress. Ugh, I need a drink. Seriously. I'll think it over from there. I check the time- 8:45pm. The party has just barely started. I walk out the bathroom door, cautiously looking around for the man. However, he was nowhere in sight. I breathed out, feeling calmer. Once again, I walk into the room, a small orchestra of violins play the distant melody of claire de lune. The soft murmuring of talking filled the room. So high class and fucking boring. I spotted an empty seat, a stool of ivory and a dark green twinge.

I sat at the bar and called for a drink of whiskey. "Here you go darlin'," the bartender says handing me the fancy glass. She smiles at me, "Let me know if you need anything else." I return the smile but stop halfway. She gives me a different impression. She's gorgeous, but she seems too watchful to be a regular bartender. Her hair was black and she had a mole (beauty mark) under her eye. Her arms were graceful with making each drink and her eyes were a shocking green. Before I could ask her something, someone leaned over and spoke to her. "Hey, baby. I'll pay you extra if you spend the night with me." He wore a black suit with a red tie. His blonde hair was messy and his face was just plain creepy.

Just where the hell is he looking? I notice him staring at her breasts and lips. I felt shivers go down my spine. "I don't need your money. Are you that damned desperate to get laid?" She chided. His face twists from friendly to enraged. He retracts his arm and slams his hand on the bar table, "I won't take no for an answer", he says, his voice becoming more and more dangerous. The girl crosses her arms and sighs, "Boys boys boys. This is why I hate you all. So forceful and when you don't get your way, you cry like a little baby. This is why I swing for the other team." The man growls, "What the hell do you mean the other team?" The girl looks at him pridefully, her arms still crossed, "It means I like women, not disappointing bastards like you." He lurches over the table and grabs her wrist, squeezing hard. She yelps in pain. "Then I guess I can teach you how a man does things," he says while licking his lips.

That's it. "Enough," I snap. Suddenly standing up, I spill my drink all over his grisly head. What a waste. That drink was so good though. Wide-eyed stares look at us with surprise. My face burns with embarrassment, but it doesn't stop me. "You think consent is a joke? God, get a grip. Regardless of class. It seems as if you have no manners," I seethe, full of anger. He releases her arm and swings to strike me, fury in his eyes. Thanks to Sam's training, I dodge it easily by evading it and punch him square in the face. He falls over, groaning with pain. The music stops suddenly. The whole room directs their attention to us. "Carry on. Pay no attention to the disruptiveness of others," a husky voice says over the microphone. I only recognize it as Ethan's and my body pleads to turn towards him. I'm betraying myself...

I ignore my desires and direct my attention to the girl. "Hey, are you alright?" She nods and smiles, "Thank you so much. You saved me from a lot of pain." Her face immediately falls. "Watch out!" I turn to see that the prick who was lying on the floor was holding a knife and was right above me... I could hear Ethan's strained voice from far away, "Cara!" I wince. There's no way I can move away in time, but I can minimize the damage. Suddenly, an arm sweeps me to the side and a tall figure had slammed the side of his hand on the attacker's neck. I hear a large crack and the attacker falls so suddenly. The audience had gotten so used to these fights that there was no reaction from them. I look up at the man who was holding me and nearly have a heart attack. I-It's Mr. Taki. "Well Princess, you seem to be attracting bad company today. We really must talk privately," he whispers in my ear. I move back aggressively and he laughs.

I spot Ethan weaving through crowds and chairs trying to get to me. His expression was clouded with worry and anger. "Let go over right now Takemura," he snarls. Taki holds me tight, not allowing me to move at all. "Oh? You mean her? What is she to you Grey? Does it anger you if I do this?" He kisses my neck while staring at Ethan and

I blush profusely. This only pisses Ethan off even more and he walks closer, his steps silent. "Bye Yuki. I'll be back." The bartender, now known as Yuki smiled gently and waved. Taki collects me in his arms princess style and runs off with me. I try to struggle out his grasp, but it does no good and I reach out towards Ethan. He runs after me but is stopped by several security guards.

We end up on the other side of the clubhouse and he leads me to the patio. It is warm out; after all, it is summertime. He sets me down beside the bottles of beer. We are alone. This is bad. He probably knows that he's supposed to be my target. He pulls me by the waist and purrs, "Well well. How should I pay you back?" I tilt my head confused, "What do you mean? I haven't done anything." He gently releases me and bows deeply. "You saved my sister from that bastard. He is known for his sexual assaults, kidnappings and abusive nature. Because he is so wealthy, he is not only powerful but has a strong connection to authorities. He is dangerous and you gave me the right reason to murder him in broad daylight," he says appreciatively.

"W-wait. You killed him?" I stammer. He rolls his eyes and I could hear the "duh" from inside his head. "Alright, you did. No one could survive that. But that is your sister?" He nods and sighs, "She gets so much trouble working here, but she has to because she's a spy." I clench at my dress and look away. I don't know what to do now. Taki raises his eyebrows at me and his hand reaches up my dress. I turn red immediately and raise my hand to hit him. His hand gently trails higher and higher up my leg. I gasp, "What the hell are you doing?" He takes the jade knife from under my dress. "I will be confiscating this for the time being. It is almost as gorgeous as you. Anyways, I know that you were sent to kill me. You may have been able to, but I would have been a hard target. However, I know Ethan sent you because he didn't know whether I was a threat or not. In fact, I was simply neutral with many connections. I don't care about other people's business. Whoever pays me the higher price, I produce." I tilt my head at him in admiration, "So you did know all along. I figured you were one of those brainless models."

"You have a lot of nerve woman," he smirks. I laugh, pulling away from him, "Be my ally then. You do owe me that favor don't you?" "Well aren't you a little opportunist? I will take you on your offer. I would make you mine, but it seems you are taken," he purrs once again. "You're right Takemura. She's mine," a sudden voice erupts from the shadows. "Ethan," I say, keeping my voice low. I wanted to yell at him, jump in his arms and hit him all at the same time, but I restrained myself. "Don't stress yourself out Grey. Evangeline and I are allies now," Taki says listlessly. Ethan was taken aback and smiles at me, "As expected Cara. Well done." Taki writes his number on a slip of paper and hands it to me along with the knife. I pray that Ethan doesn't notice. But alas, he does, "How the hell did you get her weapon?" Taki walks off before turning around one last time with a chiding smirk. "I personally received it myself." Then, he disappeared into the shadows.

"Ethan," I say and he directs his attention to me. I never fully noticed how amazing he looked. His hair was tousled and fluffy. His piercing grey eyes stared right at me. His suit was black and tight around his muscles. His white dress shirt under the suit was unbuttoned slightly. His earring on his left ear was a silver ring. He was just gorgeous.

- Ethan's POV-

Seeing her in the bar made me think different of her. I saw her in that red dress and I wanted to steal her away. She attracted admiring stares of men and the glares of jealous women. However, she had a role and that was to assassinate Takemura. He and I go way back, but his neutrality pisses me off. He allows himself to be bought with money like the cheap bastard he is. I can't allow a threat like that loose. Then I saw Cara. What the fuck is she doing now? She responded to an assault on the bartender and her words make her seem so big. Impressive. When I saw her punch the daylights out of that disgusting trash, I decided that I would never let her go. But when I saw him hold that knife above her, my heart dropped. I surged forward my body wanting to go protect her. My mind was screaming at me.

Then I saw Takemura come out of nowhere. He protected her and I couldn't even do that... Nevertheless, I rushed toward her, but that bastard took her away. Apparently, Cara saved Yuki, Takemura's sister, but still. I couldn't trust him. I lost track of him for a while and heard Cara's laugh. They were on the patio..laughing. Why do I feel super pissed off? I want to strangle Takemura.

I saw him pull Cara towards him and she pulled back shyly. I took this as my chance to come out from the shadows and I saw the glimmer and relief in her eyes. She was truly beautiful. Her lips were drawn in a glossy pout, her back was open, tempting, her eyes sparkled when any light reflected on it and her hair hung in wisps around her face. When Takemura admitted he touched her, I fumed so much. However, he hadn't harmed her and she successfully made an alliance with him.

I took her face in my hands and I kissed her hard. She looked at me breathily and my hand trailed down her back, leaving her shivering.. "Let's go home," I breathed in her ear.

BEHOLDER

Author's note: Here's a sample picture of Liam

-Cara's POV-

I hold Ethan's arm as we find the exit for the party. "Wow you two look regal," a playful voice says behind me. I glance and see Coletta, her hair mussed and her dress sleeve was torn. "God what happened to you," I gasp when I see her all disheveled. She groans, "That bitch was so annoying. She was so hard to kill." I touch her arm and Coletta winces in pain. "A fracture. I figured," I say, taking the knife out of under my dress. "Ethan. You seriously have done it this time," a shrill and clearly angry voice announces. An old woman says marching forward, her cane held in the air. "Madam Whit," Ethan says not flinching. "You goddamn bastard. How many times are you going to cause a commotion and ruin my parties?" Ethan nods apologetically, "Madam, I came with compensations. Your money will be given tomorrow. Until then, leave us alone."

The lady scowls and walks away muttering, "You better." Ethan turns to me and whispers, "I'm going to get Sam and Kyle. They're taking too long." I nod at him and smile at him. God he's so handsome. No wonder ladies were all over him. There's no way he would be interested in a girl like m-. Ethan swooped me in his arms and kissed me. It was a hard kiss that told me more would come afterward, but he departed and headed off in the opposite direction. "Well look at you lovebirds," Coletta says weakly, a smug grin on her face. I playfully bonk her on the head and use my jade knife to tear the bottom of my dress. Now I just need a splint.

I looked around frantically and spotted a wooden curtain rod by the windows. I rush over and pull it off with all my force. "God Cara. Don't wreck the whole house for me," Coletta laughs holding her limp arm. "Ethan's got money," I shoot back with a smirk. I throw the rod on the ground and place my foot on one end. On the other end, I pull up with all my force, snapping it. Quickly, I lay her arm on the rod and gently tie it with the remains of my dress. I sigh and sit down on the ground. Suddenly, I see Ethan come out with Sam and Kyle. They were injured and hobbling with the support of Ethan. He says worriedly, "Cara can you fix them?" I nod and reach for my knife. All of a sudden I hear shuffling of feet. What is that? I turn and see armed men dressed in black running down the stairway. I stand, alarmed, "Ethan!" He had already noticed. His hair was ruffled and his grey eyes stormed. His strong hands lay inside his coat, obviously on his gun. "Cara you will listen exactly to what I say," he says firmly. Coletta slumps passed out from exhaustion. Men swarm everywhere from every exit possible.

I hear a slow clap and my attention goes to the top of the stairs. The room was red, the curtains a rich yellow. The stairs were a glossy black marble, like obsidian. And there..There stood Liam. "Bravah Ethan. You successfully assassinated four of the finest villains and befriended one of the most important men in the world. Ah no that wasn't you..That was dear Miss Evangeline wasn't it?" Ethan snarls, "As if your ungrateful ass was going to do anything. You abandoned us. You-" Liam clucks disapprovingly, "Now now Tan tan. Remember. We don't talk of the past." I cradle Coletta's head in my lap, her breaths shallowing. "Ethan we don't have much time. She has a gash on her side and she's losing too much blood," I whisper. "Now like I said, Miss Evangeline. You will come with me. We have matters to discuss," Liam says interrupting. He says, taking a sharp knife from his pocket and tossing it in the air. Catching it. Tossing in the air. I shake my head with anger, "What makes you think I'm coming with you?" He stops, the knife clasps back into his hand, "What makes you think I'm asking you?" I was taken aback. Can't the bastards leave me alone.. "You aren't taking her you fool. She's mine. I fucking told you that," Ethan says his words dripping with fury.

Liam descends the stairs, men parting to give him room. "Now let's make a deal shall we? I will give you the best doctor in my organization to help your lackeys. And in return, I get to borrow Miss Evangeline here," he smiles, gesturing his hand to an old man. Ethan was thinking, his eyes darting back and forth. "Ethan. I don't have the resources to help them. Their blood loss is too much. Let me go," I muster, my heart pleading to stay. Ethan whispers harshly, "No.

There must be another way." Liam clucks and stares at his watch, "Time's up pretty boy. She's mine now." He takes out a syringe from his pocket and lunges towards me. Ethan reaches to me and the world goes black.

-Ethan's POV-

Oh God. "What the FUCK did you do," I growl, my hand revealing the gun I had hidden. "Calm down. I injected her with a type of poison that I only have the antidote to. So be a good little boy and wait your turn. Such a gorgeous woman as herself can't be kept to just one man. Isn't that right Dev?" A man nods and takes Cara into his arms. My heart was sinking and my head filled with anger. I took a step towards Liam. Guns whipped out of nowhere and were trained on me. I growl, "You better not do anything to her." Liam waves his hand dismissively. The crafty bastard. I will rip his throat out and feed him to the dogs. Liam stares at Cara, his hand caressing her face. I nearly explode. "Wow Ethan. What control this woman has over you. Make any attempt to rescue the damsel and I'll slit her throat." He struts off, the men following him and..Cara in his arms. Only one person remained behind and it was the so-called doctor. "Don't worry Mr. Grey. She is in good hands unless he's seriously interested in her," the old man reassures, his hand on Coletta's forehead. "What the hell do you mean interested?" The man stares at me like I'm an idiot. God if he anything but a doctor, I would put a damned bullet through his head. "Shouldn't it be obvious Mr. Grey? Interested as in romantically interested," he mutters in his Romanian accent.

Author's note: Sorry this chapter is a bit short. Let me know if you would like more!

PUNISHABLE

-Cara's POV-

Urgh. My head. What the hell. "You're awake Miss Evangeline," a low voice says amidst my fogginess. I try to sit up, but my joints turn to jelly. My heart was pounding rapidly and I wince. I instantly fall back onto the pillow and mattress and struggle, my body failing to respond. "Don't stress yourself too much darling. You were injected with a poison derived from hemlock and an antidote to counter it. I feel myself raging, "For what damned purpose? I could've died. Dosages of hemlock are extremely harmful to the immune system and-" Liam suddenly appears in my view and his hand is held over my mouth. "Shut up. You act as if I have no knowledge of such thing. My researchers were the ones to design this specific poison. Now get some rest again Evangeline. Right now you are far too weak. You have work to do," Liam growls as he walks out the door. I close my eyes, my breath slowing.

As soon as the door closes and clicks, my eyes snap open and I feel my wrist. I rip off the IV patch and sit up immediately. Okay. Think Cara. My mind thinks of Ethan. I yearn for his touch and his breath. Ugh. I shake off my thoughts and I slip out of the bedsheets. The room was purely white. The walls were slick quartz and I saw a table and an IV drip. I search the room, keeping my footsteps as silent as possible. Bingo. I spotted a box hidden behind the stupid aloe vera plant. I open it with eagerness. Please please please give me something. I rummage through and rip out the gauze, bandaids, ointments, and..a syringe filled with mysterious liquid. There was a tape on it that read, "Only use to detain patients". Perfect. How come I didn't notice this earlier? I was..I was wearing a hospital gown. Someone fucking changed me? Was it that fucking bastard? That-I hear a faint voice outside the door. Fuck. I kick the supplies behind the plant and jump into the bed. I closed my eyes and grasped the syringe, my heart beating so hard it felt like popping out of my chest. The door creaks open and I play dead. Jesus, it's so hot in here. I can't imagine being in this room any longer. I hear steps walk in and a deep whistling. The figure was a man humming the tune of Claire De Lune. A man of taste. I peek at him with one eye. He is faced backward, locking the door. His build was toned and could definitely beat the fuck out of me. Maybe I should wait. "Well here's sleeping beauty. Liam sure was a pain in the ass about getting her. She doesn't look all too smart either," the voice says mockingly. I hear the steps coming closer and closer to the bed. I could feel the breath wafting slightly above my face. I literally could have burst out laughing, but I knew I would die on the spot. I bit my tongue and waited. "She's still sleeping-" His voice was cut off. Why?

What he said next made my heart drop. "Why is the IV patch on the ground?" Shit. I whip out from under the bedsheets and lunge towards him. Alarmed, he pulls back and slams into the wall. "So you pretended to sleep you brat," he growls, taking off his lab coat. I move back slowly and squat low. My hands rest on the potted aloe vera. "Well too bad shorty. Size of the dog wins," he grins wickedly and walks forward, his arms up. 2 meters. 1 meter. Now! I grab the plant and slam it on his hand. He thuds to the floor and groans. I rush to him, my knees scraping the ground and I search his pockets. A knife. Beautiful. I drag him to the door where he was still dazed. I lock the door and sigh in relief. "Frank? What the hell is all that noise?" I froze up again. Oh my God. Another one? I sigh in exasperation and my knife is gripped against the man's throat. "Hey old man. Say something or I'll slit your damned throat," I whisper lowly. He smirks at me, "As if." "Frank. I'm going to open this door if you don't answer," the voice says stubbornly. I stab the man in the shoulder, twisting the hilt. The man grunts in pain and grips my hand so tightly. All of a sudden he yells, "Goddamn it Lewis. I'm in the middle of something. Come back later!" I smile with relief and slide open the cap of the syringe. "Goodnight Frank. You really whistle Claire De Lune beautifully," I whisper and his shocked face collapses as I stab the side of his neck with the needle.

There's no time. I grab the knife and take his keycard. I open the door and peek outside. I lock the door from the inside and sprint down the hallway. I then slam face-first into someone's chest. Blood drains from my face and I look up to see a well-built man sneering at me and staring at my dress. "An escapee huh. Well aren't you cute," he says peering into my face. I scowl, "Are all men as perverted as you?" I don't give him a chance to answer as I karate chop his neck and knee his groin. He collapses in pain and I run past him. I hear his weak and frustrated voice scream a code red. The white hallways bleed with the blaring colors of red and a piercing alarm. I run into a diversion of hallways and see men appearing behind me. I keep running, going left. Right. Straight. Right. I've lost count.

All of a sudden, a hand grabs my arm and whips my whole body into a room. The men running behind me pass by and a hand is kept closed over my mouth. I look at the person behind me. It's a man? He looks different than the others. His uniform was a navy blue instead of white. His face was gruesome and gnarled. I whisper, "Who are you?" He doesn't answer and his face starts beading with sweat. He begins to pant and steps towards me. Why do I feel scared? The room was dark and sunken. I stammer, taking steps back towards the opposite wall, "Why the hell aren't you answering?" He lunges towards me and whispers shakily, "God. You look so good." I shiver and I freeze up. This reminds me of the time...when.. The man's arms clasp my shoulders and slam me into the corner of the room. I fall with a thud and it nearly takes all my breath away. His hand wraps around me and his hand fiddles with the grubby strings that keep my whole dress intact. I begin shaking. I can't move I- tears begin clouding my vision. I tremble, my hands laying limp by my sides. Stop. Please. His face shoves into my neck and his slimy tongue grazes over my shoulder blades. I push him, but it doesn't do any good. His cracked and cold hands slide up my dress and up my thighs. "You smell so sweet. So damn fucking good," the man grins and says shoving his mouth onto mine. Tears spill out of my eyes. I bite him and he rears back in pain. "Please stop. Please. I can't do this anymore," I plead, holding the remnants of the dress to shield myself. His hand raises to slap me, lust and annoyance in his eyes. I flinch and I wait for the hit, but I don't feel it. I see blood spurting out of his neck and his widened eyes. The man's hands fly up to his neck and attempt to stop the blood loss. After he collapses, the figure behind him stares at me.

It's..Liam. I flinched, thinking he would hurt me for trying to escape, but he walked away and out the door. I sat there for a few minutes, my hands trembling madly and my heart beating sorrow-fully. He returns and his hand clasps a white blanket that looks as soft as a sheep's coat. I open my mouth to say something, but he shakes his head, telling me not to speak. I whimper as he stands me up. I feel like a newborn calf who can hardly walk. His hand reaches for my dress and I pull back instinctively. "I'm sorry. I won't look. Give me your dress and you can wear the blanket," he murmurs softly, his gaze gentle. I do so and I collapse to the ground, his hand grabbing my arm. He lifts me up princess style and holds me. The world goes black.

-Liam's POV-

I had been mean to this girl for a while. I never expected it would turn out like this. My heart pained for her. She was almost raped and it was a good thing I arrived on time. "Maxwell. Open the suite and get her a room. I trust she won't make any more escapes. And don't forget to clean the mess in room 130451B," I order. Maxwell salutes and sprints off. I had my eyes on her all along. I just wanted to see what qualities Ethan liked so much. She was clever, strong, and gorgeous. When she escaped the room, I followed her on all cameras and she kept off the men for a long while. I was impressed, but after a while, she disappeared off the radar. When I had searched for her, I noticed that she was sucked into a room. I had to investigate for myself. I leaned against the door and heard the conversation. However, it was alarming to hear her plead so much. I heard a gruff voice I'd never heard before and realized it was one of the men that we had been trying to catch for so long. I don't know why, but it angered me so much to hear her begging and crying. I killed the man without thinking. I looked at her face and saw trauma in her eyes. Obviously, this isn't the first time for her. I picked her up and let her rest. She was curled perfectly in my arms and I had the instinct to protect her. Ethan. I think I want her.

NEW ENVIRONMENT

A uthor's note: Here's Cara!:)
- Cara's POV-

I woke up with a start. My God. A dream! I look around, but I'm not in the blank and empty room. I'm in a room with green walls, a sweet aroma of lavender surrounds the room. I see plants all over the place. "You like them?" A pitched voice says slurring. I sit up in bed. The sheets were a purple satin. I make eye contact with a beautiful girl with red hair, piercing green eyes, and a gorgeous figure. She wears a lab coat and turns towards me, her fingers playing with the small lily intertwined in them. I slip out of bed and realize I was wearing the blanket and nothing else. I close the blanket ever so tightly and walk to the woman, wobbling. "Stop that. Your leg was injured in the scuffling," she says catching my arm when I fell. "My name is Ivy. I manage the poison and health department," she says with a straight face. Her fiery red hair bounced around her head. She leads me to the bed and lays me down. "Liam will be in soon. Just wait a bit," she said taking my temperature. She leaves the room and I'm alone again.

What happened yesterday? Flashbacks hit me and tears spill out of my eyes.

"It's okay. I'm here," a soothing voice says and I flinch. Liam sits next to me, holding a lavender stem. He sits me upright and whispers, "You're going to be okay. Change into these clothes when you're ready," he says purring. He walks out of the room and I'm left alone once again. I wait a few minutes and I get up, reaching for the clothing.

-Liam's POV-

I leave her room, closing the door behind me. I walk speedily to the room where Ivy was. She nodded towards me, "He just barely lived. We were able to revive him. But the bastard seems to be in better condition than we thought." She flips several pages in her clipboard. "Go visit him now. He's awake," Ivy says flatly. Good. I can pummel the bastard. I walk through the swinging doors, my hand trembling in anger. "Polo," I say growling. He sits up in bed, his face calm, but his eyes betraying them. They showed pure fear. "I won't say anything. Even if you torture me, I won't reveal my secrets," Polo says sneering. His stubble and mussed hair made me want to throw him into a fire to burn. "Very well," I smile, "Then you won't mind me doing this?" I grab his hand and he freezes in fear. I take the knife from my pocket and lick the blade.

He stammers, his hand trying to slip out of my grip, "I-I won't-" I slam his hand flat on the hospital bed and stab the knife into the middle of his palm. He screams painfully and groans with pain. "How about now?" Ivy bursts into the room, her brow furrowed and was obviously pissed. She stomps over to Polo and grabs his shirt. "You fucking disgusting rat. Shut the fuck up before I inject a cyanide-based poison into your bloodstream. Then you will feel blood pouring out of your eyes, pus coming out of your ears, and feel such fatigue and pain in your whole body that you want to die. You're bothering my patients," Ivy says, her voice extremely deadly and quiet. Polo shakes with fear and stares at me, his calm facade crumbles slowly. He begins running his mouth while Ivy hands me the injection that would eventually kill him. He panics and starts talking more. When he finished, I had learned three valuable things. Ace was going to make his move soon and he was going to start with Ethan. Ethan's warehouses were raided recently, but unsuccessfully. His warehouses are his source of income and he guards it better than anyone else. Lastly, Ace is back from Europe. He is gathering intel and allies.

"Well. You realized you sexually assaulted a girl yesterday," I say dangerously. I feel like punching his face inside-out. He laughs. Wrong move. "Please. If you had seen the girl, you would've done the same. Her face was stunning and her body was perfect. You shouldn't blame me. She is-" I was going to keep him completely intact, but I couldn't help it. I sliced his finger off and the bed turned into a deep scarlet. Ivy sighs behind me, "Damn. You know how hard it is to get blood out of the sheets." Polo screams bloody murder and holds up his separated finger. "Shut the fuck up," Ivy says, clearly irritated and stabs him with a sedative and he falls asleep. She bandages his finger and tells the other doctors to not give him any painkillers.

"Rico. Wrap him up and send him to Ethan as an early birthday present," I say. Rico comes over and wheels the hospital bed away. Hm. How's Evangeline doing?

-Cara's POV-

I put on the outfit. It was beautiful. It was a white pullover and a green skirt. I felt comfortable for the first time in days. How long has it been? How's Ethan? Why does my heart hurt and why am I so sad? Nevermind that. I need to find Liam. I walk out of the beautiful place, not wanting to leave. I wander the hallways and look around for walking passersby. I see a man in a lab coat wandering the hallways, "Sir? Where's Ivy?" He looks at me puzzled and says, "Who are you? I never have seen you before.." I stammer, "Erm.. I-I'm new." He leans forward into my face, "Is that so? Well, what's your name darlin'?" A hand holds my shoulder and pulls me back. "Maximus. Stop hitting on her. Does she know about your ten failed tinder dates? No? Go check up on your two patients. One is suffering from a gun wound," Ivy says blatantly. Maximus turns red and rushes off. "Sorry about him. Anyways were you looking for me, sweetheart?"

I laugh, "Yes. I wanted to tell you how beautiful your plants are. Especially the lavender ones. I wish I could have a garden like that at home. And you must be so smart too!" Ivy laughs and says sweetly, "Of course. But I read up on you Cara. You are the top of your class and definitely doctor-material. In fact you were brought here because of our shortage of doctors. Our underground hospital was raided last week and many medical workers died," she says sorrowfully. I pat her shoulder, "Of course. Tell me what to do." She beckons me to follow her and I do. I start work immediately. I was trained to do so.

-Ethan's POV-

I sit in my room frustrated. I hate not seeing her. I despise it. There must be some reason he took her. I put on the white silk robe and sigh. "Tan, you have been on edge since Cara was taken. Maybe we should get her back," Coletta says, walking into my room and sitting on my bed. I roll my eyes, "Shut up Coletta. It's none of your business," I growl. Now it's her turn to roll her eyes. "Face it, Ethan. You like her. You never acted like this with any other girl," she says smirking, "But I do have an idea why they wanted her. In fact, Thomas showed me the data and news. Liam's underground hospital ended up having sixty casualties. Most of them were nurses and doctors. Since Cara is a doctor. It seems the situation was-" The doorbell rang.

"We aren't expecting anyone. Stay back," I murmur, taking a gun from the bottom of my drawer. I knock three times in a fast pace. "Who is it?" The recipient knocks back the same way and says in a low voice from behind the door, "Tigers." I throw open the door and see a man who I knew was Rico, Liam's Henchman. He was holding a man who was clearly drugged. Pinned to his chest was an envelope. I ripped it off and read it. "Regards to you Ethan. This man tried to rape Cara. I already gave him the worst treatment, but I know you'd do worse. I leave him in your hands. Liam." I was shocked and then that shock turned to anger. I crunched the letter in my fists. "Thank you Rico. I'll handle this accordingly," I say, my voice so quiet. I grab the man and shove him to the floor. "Coletta. Put this man in the basement. I have to teach this bastard a lesson."

FORTUNE

Author's note: Hey guys! Thank you so much for your support! To be honest I started these chapters at like 2am in the morning on a Saturday. Sorry I was gone. I'll be popping in and out with these chapters! This is Ethan once again!

-Ethan's POV-

I could feel the adrenaline pumping in my veins. I was gritting my teeth and I clenched my hands. This bastard hurt her. This piece of shit. He is worth nothing. I felt a light clasp on my shoulder. I turn back and sees Coletta nodding grimly towards the chair. We were in the attic and the ceiling dripped with water, the drops echoing namelessly into the void. The man was awake and his eyes widened with fear. "I'll go before it gets bloody," she said quietly and crept up the stairs to the lively living room. I cracked my knuckles, keeping a murderous calm, "Now. What do we have here?" The man scooted back into the chair, his body trembling with fear. Mm, how fucking satisfying. I peer into his face, my arm holding the arm of the chair. "Do you know who I am?" With one swift motion, I rip the duct tape off his face and watch every bead of sweat drip down his pathetic face. His teeth chattered and his hands wildly struggled to get free. "Now. Now. There's nothing to be afraid of," I say with a smile, "I won't repeat myself. So? Who am I?" His eyes were still so wide. "Y-you're Ethan Grey," he said quietly. I put one hand in my pocket, "And you are?" He opens his mouth to speak and I grab the knife sitting in my pocket and stab it into his shoulder. "Wrong answer bastard," I say smiling. My hands cover with blood and I smile dangerously.

Hmm. 3. 2. 1. The bitch wails in pain, "Fuck! Please. Please let me go. What the hell did I even do?" I murmur in his ear, "Have you seen a short, brunette who has the most slender body?" He winces with pain and thinks long and hard. "You mean that girl from Liam's lab? She was really sexy. Like r-" I cut him off by punching his gut. He reels over in his bonds and his face deforms with pain. I cut off the ropes entangling him and he flops on the floor like a pitiful fish. I bend down and grab his hair, his head pulled forcibly up. "Get this straight in your mind you fool. That was my woman. And you know what happens to people who fuck with my woman?" His face falls in realization. I stand back up, ruffling a hand through my hair. I kick him and he bends, holding his stomach on the ground. I began to beat him, my fists punching his flesh. Blood puddled the ground and the bastard lay there, breathing hard. Ugh it's so hot. I forgot I was wearing a suit. I ripped off my tie, my button shirt breaking and the cool air hits me. "Please. Let me go," the voice below me pleads, spitting blood. I grin maliciously, "You won't make it out of this basement." His face morphs into confusion and then fear. I sighed and wrapped the tie around his mouth. He begins to scream, his body flailing. I take the syringe that came with the man and flick it, making sure there aren't air bubbles. Not that I care if oxygen gets into his bloodstream. But I want him to suffer in the best way possible. "Say Goodbye fool," I snarl.

I stab the injection into his neck and sit on the floor curiously. The man writhes in pain and foam falls from his mouth. He erupts into blood-curdling screams and lastly, shudders into nothingness. I take the handkerchief from my pocket and wipe my hands of the blood. How satisfying.

-Cara's POV-

Huh. I wonder how Ethan's doing.. "Darling. Your patient is waiting," Ivy says gently and I turn towards her shaking off my thoughts. "Yes. I'll be there!" I shove on the lab coat and take the prescripted glasses Ivy let me borrow. I put my hair into a low bun and rushed to the hospital sector of this..erm underground bunker. I ran, weaving through the many people congesting the hallways. On accident, I ram into someone, my head hitting their chest. "What the-" The voice said. "I'm so sorry," I apologize and turn to go around him. "Hey. I'm not done with you." I am suddenly pushed to the wall and a hand slams next to me, trapping me. The glasses fall off my face and I instantly drop down to grab it. However, a hand grabs it already. The soft hands put them on my face and I look up at the man. Liam? "For someone so smart, you really can be idiotic Ms. Evangeline," he scoffed. I huff and roll my eyes, "Then don't bother me," I break out of his grasp and walk away. His hand grabs my arm and wrenches me back pulling me in. "You know. For a nerd, you can be quite beautiful," he says becoming awfully close to my face. All of a sudden Ethan pops into my mind. My heart throbs. "I-I have to go," I break away again. My face was really red. Oh my God.

Author's note: So sorry for the short chapter! I am also focusing on making a podcast about depression. I was wondering if you guys would be interested?

PERSPECTIVE

Author's note: Hello! I am back sorta haha. Thank you so much for your support. The number of fans I have who ask me for more of the series makes me so happy and I am blessed to have such amazing people to make me feel like my writing is worth something so thank you from the bottom of my heart. I would also like to add this: please please PLEASE do not ask for rape scenes. This concept is extremely horrible and I do not wish it for anyone at all. I only use it in the story to show how horrifying it is for the victim and how seriously it should be taken (as per Ethan's actions last episode (what a man)). Before commenting those kinds of things, please do some research! Thank you and without further ado, here is the episode!

(Picture of Mr. Grey)

- Cara's POV -

My heart ached to see all these men and women in pain. Ace, you wretched bastard. You will pay. "Ma'am. Please. My arm is hurting," a voice panted underneath me. I didn't realize I was holding the patient's arm too tightly in my grip. My hands were white and trembling with anger. "Of course... I apologize. Would you like me to replace the gauze? The blood seems to have stuck it to your wound," I ask with concern, tipping my glasses correctly. The man, pale with pain and jaundice surrounding his eyes and mouth. The pale yellowed skin was painful to look at, but I had to help him. His black silken hair stuck to his forehead in clumped sweat. He was breathing heavily as his arm was adjusted and the wound was reopened as a result of ripping off the gauze. How long have I seen blood and gotten used to it? The crimson liquid dripped all over the floor and onto my hands. I had never been disgusted. Never. Not by blood at least. All that was in my mind was the concern for the patient. "Thank you. Really. Without you..many of us would have died," the man says with a struggle. I smile and squeeze his hand, "I'm just glad I was able to provide my support." He weakly smiles and puts his hand over mine. All of a sudden I get a flashback to my Grandpa Ji who cared for me when I was younger. He was the only one in the family who loved me so other than Axel. The patient was in his fifties and his smile was in pain but kind. "What is your name dear?" I hesitated. Should I tell him my real name? "Cara. Cara Evangeline," I say nodding.

"Miss Evangeline. You must come back. Mr. Hermin needs your assistance," a girl a few years younger than me says rushedly. I tilt my head in acknowledgment. I wipe my bloodied hands on my white coat. "I must be going now Mr...." "Erickson", the man says his hand releasing mine. He shoos me away and I smile before turning away to follow the nervous stricken girl. The hours were so long, but it was so worth it. The smiles and the laughter I received made me feel whole.

After the day was done, I sat exhaustedly in the chair. "Darling. You did well," Ivy says approvingly. I smiled tiredly, "I hope I did. Anyways what's our plan for tomorrow?" She smiles sympathetically and pats my head. I look up at her. Her red hair was tied back and the mascara of hers smudged heavily. She looked like she was going to pass out any second. "You won't be here tomorrow. You are going to relax by taking the day off. You will be returning to the Grey residence soon." With that, Ivy walked away, her hair swaying and the click of her beige heels fading slowly. I rub my head with my hand and the world slowly fades away.

I feel a rhythmic bumping. I feel the sway of wind and the coziness. I slowly open my eyes, my head all tired and out of control. "Evangeline. I cannot sit in a chair for an hour comfortably. Somehow, you really make a chair look relaxing," a deep voice says above me. I widen my eyes and notice how I was being carried by Liam. His strong arms held me gently as if they could crush me at any moment. The fresh smell of the ocean breeze was in his hair. Before I knew it I instinctively touched his hair. He looks at me gently. "The ladies cannot keep their hands off me I suppose," he boasts suddenly. I scowl and neck chop the tattooed tiger on his neck. He winces with a painful smile. "I supposed I deserved that." I look around me, "Where are you taking me? My room isn't this way.." He stares at me curiously and leans close to my ear whispering, "Where would you like me to take you?" Before I could retort, he bit my ear gently and I flail around. Yes real graceful. He mutters, "Hey wai-" We both fall to the ground and somehow I land on top of him. My face peering into his.

I immediately lose all function to speak and stammer, "T-This isn't what I meant to do. I-" He smirks at me and forces up, completely flipping me over so he's on top of me. His leg between mine and his hands on either side of my head. I stare at him, my hair messy and laid cleanly on the floor. He stares at me, his eyes trailing up and down my body.

"You! Where do you think you're looking," I stammer and raise my arms to strike him. He rolls his eyes and grabs my wrists, holding them above my head. At this point, my face is completely scarlet and I was absolutely mortified. "It seems as if you don't want me to stop," he says with a smile. I can admit he is extremely handsome, but I couldn't see myself with him at all... He leans in and I squeeze my eyes. "Ahem. Mr. Liam. Call from Mr. Grey," a monotone voice says suddenly. I glance upward to see a sharp-looking man wearing a tight black suit. Liam growls and gets up, leaving me on the ground. "Why does that bastard have to ruin everything," he says muttering, "Richard. Take Evangeline to her room. See that she is safe and well-rested." Richard nods and I follow him, looking back at Liam, whose face turns from happy to serious.

- Liam's POV -

Urgh. Not this fucker again. I stride to the call room with Ivy handing the phone to me, her eyebrow raised. "Liam," I say sighing into the phone. "The deed is done. Forget about two days from now. I want to see her tomorrow," the gravelly voice says over the line. I busily tap a pen on the oak desk, annoyance flickering in my voice, "Look Tan Tan. You have nothing to worry about. The girl is in good hands." The response was not pleasant. "Liam you will listen. You weren't good enough to fucking protect her from that bastard who nearly raped her. I want her tomorrow. If I don't get her then, you will pay." That was my last nerve. "Look Grey. We aren't fucking divorced parents. Cara can choose her damn choices. The girl is fucking smart," I retort. Grey pauses. "I fucking know that you prick. But I want her tomorrow. I'm sure she wants to see me tomorrow anyway. Know your place. She wants me. Not you," he snarls. I laugh sourly, "You sure are a possessive freak Grey."

"Mmmm. Liam? Why are you yelling so loudly at night?" Shit. She's awake. I turn towards Cara who is half asleep. "Shit. Did I wake you up, Evangeline?" She nods slightly, "Who are you on the phone with?" I tap uncertaintly with the pen on the desk again, "Ethan." Unfortunately, this makes her become 100% awake. Her eyes sparkle and she feigns interest, "Ethan?" I nod in annoyance. God, he is such a pain. I put the phone in her hands and begin to walk out of the room. Cara grabs my sleeve. She mouths the words: wait. I roll my eyes and slump into a nearby chair. Her voice says with concern, "Ethan? Oh, Gods are you okay?" I hated that. She should ask me that. "Yes kitten, I am fine. You? I will never let anything happen to you ever again," Ethan's sappy voice says over the phone. How disgusting ugh. And I have to listen to this? Ridiculous. After she was done with the phone, she hands it back to me and kisses my cheek. Huh? She mouths the words: Thank you. You're amazing. As she leaves the room, I feel like I'm on top of the world. Ethan's bored voice says, "Hello?" I matter of factly put the phone to my ear and sigh, "Wow isn't a cheek kiss from Cara the best?" I could feel Ethan stiffening over the phone. "Now hold on Liam I-" I hang up the phone, smiling for the rest of the night.

- Cara's POV -

I wake up and see Ivy tending to the lavender flowers in my room. She says in a sad tone, "So today you leave then?" I nod and hug her; her eyes widen in surprise. "I will miss you," I say my face buried in her arms. "I will miss you too darling. Now hurry and get ready. It seems Grey is almost here." I run out of the room and change to get ready. On my way to the bathroom, Liam smiles and says, "Ivy was too bashful, but she gave you loads of flowers to take home." I smile and rush aways. Ivy has such a kind heart. After I was done getting ready, I headed towards the plaza where Ethan was.

- Ethan's POV -

Maybe I overdressed a bit much.. I never dressed quite as nice for any other woman... No matter. Kitten will be happy to see me. But what the hell? She kissed Liam, that snake on the cheek. Jealousy overtook me. Before I had left the mansion, Coletta teased me for wearing the nicest suit I owned. Was it too much? I looked in a nearby mirror. I was clean-cut and I was wearing a white suit. My hair was a pompadour cut and gelled back. "Ethan?" I turned to see my beautiful angel. Cara. Her hair was slicked back and she wore a modern kimono cardigan. Her hair had a lavender flower in it and she looked at me like....that. It's almost like I wanted to devour her...She rushed into my arms and I hug her tightly. "Never leave me amor," I mutter in her hair. She nods silently. I look up to see Liam looking at me disapprovingly. I also spot Ivy spying on us, her attention mostly on Cara. How annoying. To see Liam so smug like that. Hm. I grasp Cara closer to my body and she flinches in surprise. I part her hair revealing her neck and I suck. She frantically whispers into my body, patting my shoulders, "Ethan?? What the hell are you doing? Not in public!" I look up at Liam while giving her that hickey. I stare at him directly and he stiffens in anger and walks away. Like I said before, Liam. She's mine.

Author's note: Please check out my new upcoming series: "The Butler"!! Thank you so much!

HOME SWEET HOME

Ethan's POV - God I missed her. How long was it since I've
seen her last..? When I saw her I couldn't keep my hands off.. I
held her and I felt her collapse in my arms. She has gone through so
much. Kitten is stronger than she thinks I have to give her points
for that. I noticed Liam behind her huffing and his hands in his
pockets solemnly. God that bastard. Time for him to taste his own
medicine. I parted Cara's hair. She whispered faintly, "Ethan? What
are you doing?" I bit her to keep her quiet and I could feel her skin
getting hot. Hmm. Yeah that's my girl. I start to suck on her sweet and
delicate skin. Her face blossoms into a crimson rose and she blushes
furiously. God she was like a antelope in the jaws of a lion. "Ethan.
Not right now.. Not in public!" I ignore her and continue to stare
at him. I grasp Cara's waist and draw her in closer to my body. Liam
notices and stares at me dead in the eyes with a foul look. How fitting.
I whisper in her ear, "Are you ready to come home?" She nods and
keeps her head in my chest, covering her red face in embarrassment.

"You know Grey. You've got some nerve," a sharp voice says and the click of heels wanders closer and closer. "Oh. Ivy. It's always a pleasure to see you again," I laugh. Ugh I remember her. She was one of the women I hooked up with a year ago at the gala party. She is extremely intelligent and dangerous, but too prideful and..not my taste. "Every time you show your face around here it really downs the whole mood," Ivy says rolling her eyes. She takes off her glasses in one fluid motion and placed them in her lab coat pocket. "You know. They should call you poison ivy" I smirk. She really is an annoying woman. "Don't you start," she retorts, "I'm only here to see Cara off." I glance from her to Cara. "Don't worry. The flowers will be taken care of I trust that," I say. She nods her head. "Goodbye Evangeline. I'll see you soon. Maybe this time you won't be with such....undesirable company," Liam says pausing with scorn. Cara smiles uneasily, "You have treated me well Liam. I do hope to see you again."

We leave the compound and my heart starts beating. Fast and hard. We approach my private jet casually sitting on the runway. The jet was painted completely black and had gold trim. Obviously suited to my style. Again, I felt the pain. God what is wrong with me? "Timothy hand me the pills," I say clutching my chest. My bodyguard hands me a bottle and I carefully slide out two clear pills. My bodyguards get into their cars and we are the only ones (besides the pilots) entering the jet. I swallow the pills and tuck the bottle in my pocket. "Now what the hell are you doing?" Cara's voice says next to me. I peer down at her and bend to her level. "I'm taking medication darling."

We head up the steps and she leads first. We sit down on the jet and she scowls, "What do you mean medication. What is wrong with your heart?" The plane takes off at high speeds. Kitten looks out her window.

She is wearing a sheer and light white dress. The material is so fragile that if it caught on anything it would rip... She turns to me, her beautiful hazel eyes glaring into mine. I raise my eyebrow. Oh? "You cannot take medication without consulting me," she says poking me on the nose. I lean closer to her, "Well doctor. It seems I am feeling warm and dangerous. Are those symptoms of a deadly disease?" She pushes backward against the wall of the jet, her hands grasping them. She loses all function for words, "E-Erm. How warm?" I move even closer taking off my jacket and unbuttoning the top half of my shirt. "Extremely warm," I murmur. She smiles with lust glinting in her eyes. "Then I have to give you some medicine," she whispers putting her hands around my neck.

I grab her neck and kiss her hard. She returns it. I grab the front part of her dress and tear it. Like I expected, it tore quite easily. I steady my hand and put my hand on her neck, slightly choking her. She moans in pleasure. I felt more desire. I wanted her. She was mine. I bit her neck and gave her hickeys spotting all around her top half. She moaned softly in my ear and her hands gripped my shoulders. Hard. I sink lower and lower down her body. My lips feeling every inch of her. "Don't you forget. You're mine. I will kill anyone who ever tries to take you away from me again," I breath into her chest. She moans quietly and whispers, "I'm yours." I suck on her chest and bite softly.

The sounds she made were so heavenly. So satisfying. I just wanted to devour her. I slipped my finger in, her moans becoming slightly louder and louder with every thrust I did. She sighed into my hair and hand her nails scratched my back like she was clinging to me. Her hair was in a messy array and her body was so warm.

Then I put it in. Oh her voice was music to my ears. I thrust it harder and harder. She gasped so loudly and covered her own mouth to suppress her moans. Unfortunately I didn't make it easier for her. I picked her up and slammed her against the wall. She was thrusting it inside her rhythmically and was breathing wisps of cinnamon. She moaned in my ear, making me go faster, sweat beaded my forehead. I wanted her more. "Mmm. More. Ethan more," she breathily sighed into me as I slammed into her. I held her neck and I went faster. Her sighs became sharper and I could feel her tightening around me. God it feels so good. I moaned right inside her ear. I kissed her neck and thrusted harder and harder. At this point she was screaming. It went on and on. Suddenly she gasped and her body convulsed. She shook so much and her eyes rolled up. Her tongue was out and I kissed her. Saliva strung from both of our mouths and she sighed satisfyingly into my neck. I held her in my arms and she never let go. Out of all the women I had sex with. It was heaven with her.

Printed by BoD™in Norderstedt, Germany